MAELSTROM

BROKEN TIDES | BOOK THREE

MAELSTROM

BROKEN TIDES | BOOK THREE

CATHERINE JONES
PAYNE

To Nivho—
Go deep!
Catherine J Payne

FATHOM INK™

MAELSTROM

Published in the United States by Fathom Ink Press, Robinson, Texas.

This is a work of fiction. Any names, characters, places, events, or incidents are either the product of the author's imagination or are used fictitiously. Any similarities or resemblance to actual persons, living or dead; events; or places is entirely coincidental.

Visit www.fathominkpress.com for more information.

ISBN (paperback) 978-1-946693-09-9
ISBN (ebook – EPUB) 978-1-946693-10-5
ISBN (ebook – MOBI) 978-1-946693-08-2

Cover Design: Kirk Douponce, Dog Eared Design.
Interior Design: Chris Bell, Atthis Arts LLC.
Ebook Formatting: Kella Campbell, E-Books Done Right.
Author Photo: Steven Noreyko.

Visit the author at www.catherinejonespayne.com

Facebook: catherinejonespayneauthor
Twitter: @cjonespayne
Instagram: catherinejonespayne

For Stephanie, my bestie, my partner in crime, my stalwart companion on this crazy writing journey.

ONE

They've taken Benjamin.

Aunt Junia's frantic words churned in my mind. It couldn't be true. It wasn't true.

But nothing could change the fact that George lay dead on the floor in front in me. George, who'd been a second father to me—my only father for the last three years. Aunt Junia had been bound and gagged but left alive, presumably so she could relay the awful truth that they'd abducted my little brother.

Nausea roiled my stomach. I couldn't think, couldn't speak, couldn't formulate a plan. My urchin was missing.

Alexander swam up behind me and placed his hands on my shoulders. "We'll get him back," he murmured. "I promise."

Mother was already reaching for her cloak. "Jade, get your aunt out of that netting. And I need you to stay here in case a message comes. If they want money, we'll pay it. Any amount. Promise them. Give them everything in this house. If they have some other demand, come to me at once. Tell me what I need to do."

"Where are you going?" My voice cracked.

"To court," she said, "to inform the crown prince of the situation. We'll mobilize the inspectors and the Guard. We'll have him home safe before sundown."

Through the window behind Mother, I could see the first

hints of sunset descending on the city, bathing its rippling surfaces in a faint pink light. The numbness creeping into my heart told me Mother's assessment was wildly optimistic. But what else could we do?

"Okay," I finally managed.

Alexander's arms moved from my shoulders to wrap around my body. He rubbed my trembling arms.

Time seemed to freeze as a shoal of thoughts swam through my head.

My smart, funny, sarcastic brother was missing. And, for now at least, there was nothing I could do about it.

I bit my lip until I tasted blood.

They wanted Aunt Junia to tell us. That meant they wanted to use him as leverage. That meant we had a chance.

And we'd do anything to get him back.

A deadly calm settled over me. We'd move sky and sea until Benjamin was safely back home. I'd swear it on my father's bones.

And even though Benjamin's disappearance scared me more than anything I'd ever faced, I wouldn't curl in on myself or hide like a fish. The stakes were too high.

I turned to Ti and Alexander. "Alexander, go with Mother to court. Two will be safer in the canals than one. Senator, you'll need to stay here."

Senator Ti nodded her assent. As a harpy, she'd be unsafe in Thessalonike even on the most stable of days. She'd only come here to advocate for her city Marbella, which had been invaded by Neptunian warriors. I didn't know what she'd do if she was unable to return home. Thessalonike certainly wasn't about to relinquish its prejudices and welcome her.

Sometimes I hated this city.

A'a, the baby webbed-foot dragon I'd recently adopted, chittered from the other side of the room, and I swam in the direction of the noise. He was tucked in the corner, curled in on himself, his pupils wide. I scooped him up, set him on my shoulder, and scratched the top of his head. He wrapped his tail around my finger, and the touch grounded me. Calmed me. I had to hold together. Once we got Benjamin back, there would be plenty of time to fall apart.

"I'll help you untie your aunt," Ti said. "And we can wrap his body." She nodded at George.

Piercing pain stabbed my heart, and I drifted back across the room, my hand on A'a's back.

Not George.

But I'd seen death before, and I'd known at a glance that he was gone.

And once again, nothing would ever be the same.

I gave a half-hearted shrug. "Thank you. I . . . I really do appreciate it. It's hard to wrap my head around it all. I can't . . . " My voice cracked, and I shrugged, my chin lifted high.

Ti's eyes softened, and she reached out and squeezed my shoulder. I reached up and placed my hand on her wrist, wincing a little. My wrist still hurt from being twisted at the ambassador's house.

Alexander brushed up against me as he and Mother swam to the door and disappeared into the canal. I bolted the lock behind them, wondering dully how the intruders had gotten in.

Aunt Junia stared fixedly at the wall, as if willing herself to wake up from a terrible nightmare.

I didn't know what to say. "Let's get you out now," I finally managed.

Aunt Junia remained silent while Ti and I untangled the knots that bound her to the hammock chair. The first two knots came out easily, but my fingers slipped on the third. I bit my lip and tugged at the knot again. It held fast, as if determined to spite us. I tried to loosen it from one side and then the other.

"Depths," I hissed.

Ti glanced over at the knot. "That one's tight. Grab a blade from the kitchen. It'll be faster than undoing it by hand."

I wanted to yell back that I didn't want to use a blade, that I wanted to put everything back the way it was without cutting the ropes, but I held my tongue. None of this was Ti's fault, and there was no point in taking out my anger and grief on her.

With a growl in the back of my throat, I darted across the room and down the corridor toward the kitchen. When I was out of sight of Ti and Aunt Junia, I leaned my forehead against the coral wall. For the first time since I'd left Marbella, no eyes were on me, and I let my emotions finally overwhelm me. Silent sobs wracked my shoulders, and I sank to the floor.

So much had happened, and there hadn't been time to process any of it. There still wasn't. I had to stay strong. We had to release Aunt Junia. Take care of George's body. Get Benjamin back. *And find Pippa,* I realized.

Last I'd seen her, she'd been at my house, which could be a target overnight. We needed to bring Pippa here to Aunt Junia's.

Not that Aunt Junia's was safe anymore.

Pull yourself together, Jade, I chided. I drifted up off the floor and found a kitchen blade lying on the table next to a few pieces of crab and a pile of seaweed. My lip quivered. George had been working on dinner. He must have heard the commotion in the front of the house and gone to investigate . . .

I grabbed the blade and whirled around to return down the corridor. Aunt Junia was still looking blankly at the opposite wall.

"Aunt Junia," I murmured, resting my hand on her arm. "We're here. We're getting you out."

She stirred, and her eyes flickered over to me. "I'm so glad you're back," she said, her voice soft and mournful.

I gave her a sad smile. "Me too."

I grasped the knot and sawed at it with the blade, but a twinge of pain shot through my injured wrist. With a huff, I handed the blade to Ti.

"Are you alright?" Ti asked, glancing down at my hands.

I almost laughed. "Of course not. But my wrist will be fine. It's just a little sore. One of the anti-monarchist skubs twisted it."

Ti pursed her lips. "Take care of it. You'll want all your strength in the days ahead."

She sliced through the netting with expert precision, and together we eased Aunt Junia up off the chair. Aunt Junia blinked several times and stared at George's body.

"Do you need to lie down?" I asked.

She clenched and unclenched her hands, then rolled her wrists in circles. "No," she said faintly. "No, I don't want to be alone."

I pulled her against my chest. She'd been looking more and more frail in the recent years as her sickness—what she'd recently discovered to be enervia—ate at her strength. Until recently, I'd been able to pretend that nothing was changing. But the constant pain sapped her energy and depleted her emotional reserves.

I counted to ten in my head and then shifted away and cleared the shreds of netting from her hammock chair. "Let's get you sitting down."

Gently grasping her arm, I moved to help her into the chair, but she balked, tension infusing her muscles.

"What is it?" I asked.

She shook her head, gaze fixed on the chair. "Not that one, child. I can't."

"Not which one?"

"Not the one they tied me to."

All at once, I understood. The trauma was too fresh. I shifted direction, and she let me help her into another hammock chair on the far side of the room. Then I sank to the floor next to her and reached out to hold her hand.

Ti moved alongside the wall, inspecting the windows. "They came in here," she said from the far side of the room. "They broke through this one."

I looked up at Aunt Junia. "What do you remember? Can you think of any more details? Even if they're small?"

"I think I told your mother everything," murmured Aunt Junia. "There were a half-dozen of them. I didn't see any of their faces in the rush. Their wraps were kelp, I think."

I chewed my lower lip. "I'm so sorry, Aunt Junia, but can you think it through moment by moment? See if there's anything that might have slipped your mind?"

Aunt Junia screwed her eyes shut but then shook her head. "No, child, I'm sorry. It all happened so fast."

"That's okay," I said, my voice soft. "You just rest. We'll be right here."

"I have a tincture in my room," she said. "Could you bring it to me?"

She meant the puffer fish extract the physicians had given her for the enervia. I'd seen it earlier when I'd gone into her room to look for a cloak. I squeezed her hand and eased myself upward and then hurried down the corridor to her room.

We'll get him back. We'll get him back. We'll. Get. Him. Back.

I rubbed my temples as I ducked through the privacy screen into Aunt Junia's room and swam to her sleeping hammock. With a small flare of my gills, I picked up the vial and stared at it, the undeniable evidence that her disease was progressing more quickly than I'd thought possible.

A'a dug his claws into my shoulder, as though he could sense my anxiety and was alarmed by it. "We're going to be okay," I murmured.

Maybe if I kept telling him that, I'd eventually believe it myself.

Then I turned around and fled back down the corridor to the front of the house where she was sitting.

"Here." I held the bottle near her gills and unscrewed the top for just a moment, letting a tiny bit of the tincture dissipate into the water.

I thought about taking a little myself—Mother often kept some around for my anxiety attacks—but I wanted to keep all my wits about me. There was no telling what we'd have to face in the hours ahead.

I replaced the cap and set the vial down in Junia's hammock chair. Then I turned to Ti. "Let's take care of his . . . body." I tilted my head toward George, and my throat tightened. "At least find something to cover him with."

"Take some of the cloaks down from my wardrobe," Aunt Junia said.

I nodded, biting my lip until I winced from the pain. I returned to Aunt Junia's room, opened her wardrobe, and pulled down a handful of everyday cloaks that didn't seem too feminine for George's taste. He'd been subdued and unfussy in life. We'd let him rest in dignity until the inspectors arrived.

When I returned to the front room, Ti had arranged the body—crossing his arms over his chest and tucking his tail to the side so his fin extended back up almost to his waist. As I moved across the room, she spread out his feathery fin so that it lay flat on the floor.

I came up to her side and sank down next to her. Blinking rapidly, I reached up and gently closed his eyes. Then I pulled one cloak from the pile and laid it over his tail. My eye twitched as I spread another over the upper half of his body, covering his face last of all.

"Goodbye," I whispered, my chin quivering. "Go in peace."

Ti placed a hand on my upper back. "I'm so sorry."

I threaded my fingers through my hair. "We won't let

7

him die in vain. We won't let any of this happen for nothing. Not Marbella. Not Benjamin's kidnapping. None of it."

"What do you plan to do?" Ti asked, tapping her sharp fingernails on the floor.

I floated upward and swam to the other side of the room, then turned and paced to the far wall. "I don't know yet. We have to focus all our energy on getting Benjamin back first."

"Your brother?" Ti asked.

I nodded. "Younger brother."

"You must feel especially protective toward him, then."

A knocked sounded at the door, and I bolted over to open it.

"Wait!" choked out Aunt Junia.

I whirled around.

Ti nodded. "Make them identify themselves first."

Right. I nodded. Make sure it wasn't a mob of anti-monarchists come to finish what they'd started. After all, I'd been a repeat target of their violence.

I swam to the door more slowly and called through the crack in the frame, "Who is it?"

"Jade? It's Orua," came a female voice. "I have Inspector Kalos with me."

With shaking hands, I unbolted and swung open the door. "Orua!" My face crumpled, and I flew toward her and hugged her close. "Thank you for coming."

We really hadn't known each other very long—just since I'd started preparing for the trip to Marbella—but we'd faced a dragon attack, the loss of a comrade, a flight from a besieged city, and a skirmish with a group of anti-monarchists at each other's sides. I felt a kinship with her that I didn't feel with many other mer.

I drew back and beckoned both of them inside. "Mother sent you?"

The inspector nodded, his sharp eyes taking in every detail of the spacious room, skimming over Ti as if she weren't even present, and landing on A'a. I stared at him until his gaze shifted away, and then he seemed to note George's body on the floor.

"I'm here to take statements," he said. "Two of my compatriots will be here soon to collect the body. What's the full name of the deceased?"

"Georgios Cadopolos."

The inspector nodded, pulling a thin tablet from a sheaf strapped to his side. "And he works for your family, Lady Cleo said?"

"Yes." My voice broke. "He's been with us since I was quite small. And he was friends with my father even before that."

"Did he have any enemies that you know of?"

I looked down at George and realized that the edge of one of his fingers was sticking out from beneath the cloaks we'd laid over him. It felt disrespectful, somehow, and I moved forward and shifted the cloak over his whole hand.

"No," I said when I pulled back up. "I don't think he had any enemies. But we do. They took my brother."

The inspector nodded. "I'm, of course, aware of the turmoil in the city, and the previous assassination attempt. We are working on the safe return of your brother, but given the chaos, the resources we can devote to the search are slim. This makes it even more important to make sure we're tracking the right mer."

I bristled at his statement. "It's the anti-monarchists. I'm sure of it," I spat. "They murdered my father. They tried to kill me twice. The rest of my family, too."

They're taking everything away.

Yes, I'd lost faith in the monarchy as of late. But I certainly wasn't going to embrace those murderers either. Rage stirred in me, churning just below the surface.

The inspector nodded. "Did you witness the murder and abduction?"

9

I shook my head and gestured at Aunt Junia. "My aunt was here at the time. She saw it."

The inspector took in her pallid face and the vial at her side.

"The puffer fish extract is from the physicians," I said. "For her enervia. She's not an addict."

He shrugged. "If you say so."

I wanted to snarl at him for impugning Aunt Junia, but I held myself back. We had bigger problems than a slight.

The inspector swam to Aunt Junia and began asking her a series of questions in a low, calm voice.

Orua moved from window to window, inspecting the locks. She reached the window Ti had pointed out earlier. "They came in over here," she called. "I'll have someone come replace the shutters right away. And we're going to assign you two guards, day and night."

I wanted to retort that I didn't trust the guards not to be loyal to the anti-monarchists. Not after all the discontent in their ranks.

She must have read the expression on my face. "I'll be on duty for one shift per day, and I'll hand-pick the others. As soon as Maximus is back, we'll put him on the rotation."

My gaze softened. "Thank you. Do you know if Maximus knows about his brother?"

Orua tilted her head. "Andronicus? What about him?"

"That . . . the king had him killed?"

Orua's mouth fell open. "I . . . had not heard about that." She stared at the wall. "They weren't close."

I pulled A'a down off my shoulder and cradled him to my chest. "The king had him sunk off the drop-off without a trial. Made all the anti-monarchists watch."

Orua stiffened. "He . . . did what?"

I nodded grimly.

With a huff, she said, "Well, no wonder they rebelled."

The inspector shot her a sharp look but said nothing.

Orua had betrayed her doubts about the king's leadership on our trip to Marbella, but even I was surprised that she'd said it so openly here in the city.

I scrambled for a response, but she continued, "I have no doubts of Max's loyalty—he's the best of any of us—but we'll need to take him off duty for a few weeks to give him a chance to come to terms with the loss. I guess we won't have him on your rotation after all." She paused as if in thought. "But I know plenty of other guards who'll do an admirable job. We'll make sure you're all safe."

Grief welled up in my chest. "Let's focus on my brother for now. Then we can worry about everything else."

CHAPTER

TWO

Mother and Alexander—accompanied by four members of the Royal Mer Guard—arrived home just after dark, and the lines on Mother's face were deeper than I'd ever seen them before.

"Any news?" I asked from where I sat against the wall.

Alexander shook his head. "Not yet. But they'll have demands. It's the only thing that makes sense. We should hear from them soon."

I'd been telling myself that since the moment I'd heard that Benjamin was missing. I ran my fingers over the rough coral wall to try to steady my thrumming heart.

"The inspectors and the best of the Guard are searching for him," said Mother, approaching me. "I'm going home in case they send word there."

She sank to the floor beside me, clasped my hand, and looked into my eyes. "Will you be alright here? I'd like you to stay with Aunt Junia. The stress has been aggravating the enervia, and I'm sure you've seen how she's deteriorated."

I set my jaw. "When this is all over, I'm sure I'll collapse, but we'll all stay strong for now. We don't have any other choice."

Her gills flared. "No. No, we don't."

Mother dropped my hand, turned without another word, and left with two of the soldiers. I willed myself to relax. The attempt was useless, I knew, but I couldn't afford to run out of energy. Not with the threats pushing in on us from every side.

Benjamin's kidnapping. The king's assassination. And the Neptunians still out there.

Alexander rubbed the back of my neck. "You need to get sleep, Jade. You're exhausted."

"I can't sleep," I said, my voice hoarse.

"You need to try. Use some of the puffer fish tincture if you have to. You will be of more use to him if you are refreshed tomorrow than if you spend all night swimming from one end of the room to the other."

"He's right," said Aunt Junia.

I jumped, startled. I hadn't realized she was listening.

"Take some." Aunt Junia extended the bottle.

"I agree," said Ti.

I hesitated, thinking through each sensation in my body. My pounding heart. The cold, heavy dread pressing all the way down my arms. The burning, pulsing sea urchin of fear in my chest. The nausea. Yes, I was panicking. It was time to accept the tincture.

I swam to Aunt Junia and took the bottle. Holding it up to the side of my head, I opened the tincture just for a moment and wafted it toward my gills. Then I closed it again and handed it back.

No sooner had my fingers relinquished the bottle than I felt the changes in my body. A subtle, profound calming. The nausea faded; the dread lessened its hold.

I loved Benjamin so much. And I needed to sleep in case I had the opportunity to help get him back.

"A little more," I said, reaching for the bottle again. This time I held it up to the gills on the other side of my head, and as I handed back the bottle, I thought I might have a chance at sleeping after all.

Aunt Junia studied my face, though her expression still seemed almost blank. "Oh, my dear. We're all shipwrecks, aren't we? Why don't you take the second-to-last room toward the back. On the right. Try to rest."

"Okay," I whispered.

Alexander kissed my forehead. "I'll sleep, too," he said, "in one of these hammock chairs out front. If anyone comes in, they'll have to go through me."

The thought didn't comfort me, but I whispered, "Thank you," and gave him another hug before I swam down the corridor toward one of Aunt Junia's spare sleeping chambers.

After I ducked through the privacy curtain, I took in the room. I'd stayed here before on a handful of occasions growing up. It was small but comfortable, with a hammock on one side and a small desk and hammock chair on the other. The window was normally open to the small gap between Aunt Junia's house and her next-door neighbor's, but today the shutters were closed throughout the whole house. I checked that they were firmly secured before I settled down onto the hammock.

Closing my eyes, I let the events of the day wash over me. What a horrible, horrible day. So much fear. So much loss. I'd been relieved when we'd finally made it home to Thessalonike, but it had turned into a nightmare.

Even with a double dose of puffer fish tincture clouding my mind, it still took a long time to fall asleep.

⌒

A loud rapping sounded on the door late in the afternoon the next day, and I startled, my hand clutching the kitchen knife I was using to shred a pod. Was Mother back? Or was this the news we'd hoped for, and feared?

"I'll get it," I called, racing from the kitchen to the front room. The two members of the Guard who had stayed with us hovered behind me as I unlatched and opened the door.

A boy of about ten years floated just outside. He extended a tablet to me. "Someone paid me a drachma to bring this tablet to this house."

The taller of our guards barked, "Who? What did they look like?"

The boy shrugged. "A merman."

I bit down hard on my lip. "Do you remember anything about him? Please. It's important."

The little boy glanced down the canal. "I don't think I should say."

I reached out and gently grabbed his arm. "Just one or two details. Anything."

"Yellow hair. Young." He jerked away from my grasp and darted down the canal.

The shorter soldier, a merman with aqua hair and a sharp nose, plunged into the canal in pursuit. He followed the boy around the corner and out of sight, and I floated back and looked at the tablet he'd given me.

My hands trembled.

It was wrapped in a thin fabric, and I untied the knot with shaking fingers, ignoring the twinge in my wrist.

I glanced at Ti and Alexander before staring at the script and reading aloud, "The boy will be returned safely in exchange for a sworn, public statement from the new king that a senate will be formed in Thessalonike. This senate will be elected by the people and will govern alongside the king as an equal power. If this demand is not complied with, the boy will be sunk alive off the drop-off. You have three days."

Nausea roiled my stomach. There was no way in the depths the king would comply with the demands of these skubs. The edges of my vision grew blurry.

Perhaps I'm wrong. King Stephanos would never comply, but might Elias be persuaded?

Without a word, I grabbed a cloak off the back of a hammock chair and tucked it over my head. With a nod at Alexander, I darted for the door. He followed close behind me. The soldier moved to stop me, but I held up the tablet. "Mother needs to see this. Stay with the senator and my aunt. Keep them safe. Please."

The soldier nodded his assent. No doubt he didn't want to answer to Lady Cleo if I accused him of trying to keep the information from her.

"Don't let her get hurt," he muttered to Alexander. "It'll be my head on the line."

Alexander rolled his eyes. "I know better than to try to float in her way when she's set her mind to do something."

I reached for his hand, and we slipped out of the house. Our canal was nearly empty—none of the nobles were eager to stir outside their homes in these threatening days. Even the surface of the water above us was choppy and tumultuous, as if the sea shared our fear and anger.

Storm season is coming early this year.

We turned onto an equally empty canal lined with elegant homes made of bright coral, and I wondered if the anti-monarchists were gathering outside the palace. We'd need to get the news to the king—*the crown prince*, I corrected myself—as we worked out a plan to get Benjamin back.

My gills flared. *How will we ever get Elias to agree to such demands?*

But maybe we wouldn't have to. *Maybe the inspectors will find Benjamin before our time runs out.* I had to hope for that.

Two more turns brought us to my house, and my heart leapt into my throat when I saw it, sitting there full of thousands of memories from back when everything was normal.

I surged forward, down the path to the front door, past a subdued coral garden teeming with tiny seahorses.

"Mother!" I banged on the door. "Mother, we've got something!"

Mother swung the door open and ushered us inside. "A ransom note? What do they want?"

I proffered the tablet without another word.

Mother skimmed it without a visible reaction. When she finished, she looked up at me, her jaw tight.

"Well?" I said. "What can we do?"

She shook her head and hissed, "Idiots."

I'd never heard such venom in her voice.

She threw the tablet down toward the floor, and it turned end over end as it sank. "Do they think that I have the power to manipulate Elias into such a decision?"

I reached for Alexander's hand and took in his comforting presence. "Surely, there's something we can do. To play their game. Outmaneuver them."

Mother dragged her fingers through her hair. "Yes. We will. We have to."

"Should we bring the tablet to Elias?" Alexander asked.

Mother was swimming back and forth across the room with rhythmic, determined strokes, one hand on the back of her neck. "I have to think, children."

On her third loop across the room, her head snapped upward. "Yes. I'll take it to Elias."

"What's your plan?" I asked.

Determination glinted in her eyes. "The less you know, the better."

⌣

I crossed my arms. "You're not traveling by yourself. Not with everything that's going on." *Not after our family's been torn apart.*

Mother scoffed.

"You're being foolish," I said.

She unlatched the door, the tablet tucked under one arm. "You sound just like me."

"Well, *you* sound just like *me*."

She squinted at me, her brow crinkled. "What the depths are you talking about?"

I slapped my fin against the floor. "You say I'm stubborn and reckless. Where do you think I got it from?"

I couldn't read the glint in her eye.

Alexander shot me a look. "Be more respectful," he mouthed.

"What was that?" Mother asked.

"Nothing." Alexander shifted uncomfortably.

Mother opened the door. Our canal still lay empty.

"You can't stop us from coming with you." I reached for my cloak. "Besides, it's getting late."

"Then come," she spat. "We don't have time to waste on squabbling. Your brother is in trouble."

"I know that," I muttered.

We had three days. Three days to find Benjamin or convince the anti-monarchists to release him.

Where would they be keeping him? I wracked my brain.

In the city, likely. Especially since no one knows when the Neptunians will arrive.

That narrows it down.

I darted out the door, Alexander at my side. Mother closed and locked it, and we set off down the canal, moving as quickly as we could.

The Guard have been on high alert because of the Neptunian threat. They couldn't have taken him over the wall.

Then my heart sank. Maybe they'd tunneled underneath it. As I'd learned recently, situations were rarely as simple as we wanted them to be.

We couldn't assume that they'd been unable to smuggle him out of the city. And if they'd taken him to the reef, he could be anywhere. There were countless places to hide in the coral, and if they'd taken him to the kelp forest or beyond . . .

No, we needed to convince the anti-monarchists to release him.

Which meant we needed a plan—a solution if we couldn't persuade Elias to cooperate with their demands.

Because the more I thought about it, the more I felt sure he *wouldn't* cooperate with their demands.

I chewed the inside of my cheek. "What else would be as valuable to the anti-monarchists as the promise of a senate?"

Mother glanced at me. "You're asking the wrong question."

I tilted my head, flicking my fin harder. "What's the right question?"

"What's more valuable to the anti-monarchists than Benjamin?"

A rush of clarity overwhelmed me. Maybe all wasn't lost yet.

The nobles' houses went by in a blur as I turned the problem over and over again in my head.

But my thoughts were tumultuous, and I couldn't settle on any obvious solutions.

Maybe we should just wipe them out.

My own vehemence surprised me. I shook my head to clear away the vindictive thoughts. A massacre wouldn't get us any closer to finding Benjamin, and I'd already rejected the current of hatred and vengeance. I wouldn't let the anti-monarchists turn me into something I wasn't. If we used their own tactics against them, what would that make us?

No, there had to be another way.

There was always another way.

THREE

Mother, Alexander, and I tumbled into the imposing court at full speed, without the usual guarded solemnity appropriate to the room. Throughout the cavernous space, etchings of the great stories of the city's past were carved on the tall stone walls, except directly to our right, where a series of doors led into smaller rooms for more private discussions.

Elias's head jerked up when we entered. He sat at the far end of the room, in a hammock chair just beneath the throne—he'd take the throne for the first time at his official coronation.

The guards surrounding him glanced toward us but hardly tightened their grips on their weapons.

"Cleo," said Elias, his voice tense and uncertain. "You're back already."

Mother drew herself upward, projecting a confidence I couldn't summon in myself as we glided forward together. "The demands have arrived, Your Highness."

Out of the corner of my eye, I caught sight of Prince Theo, Elias's younger brother, deep in conversation with Advisor Galena. I offered him a little wave, and he gave me a tight-lipped smile.

A sympathetic smile, I decided.

A twinge of nausea washed over me, and I wondered if Theo thought Benjamin was already lost to us.

I turned my attention back to Elias, who had wordlessly extended his hand toward the tablet.

After a slight hesitation, Mother swam the rest of the distance and handed it to him.

Elias's brows drew closer together as he skimmed it. When he finished, he scoffed. "This is preposterous. They can't imagine we'd agree to such a request. No child is worth the whole order."

From my vantage point behind her, Mother didn't appear to flinch, though I knew magma must have been flowing through her veins.

"Perhaps," she said, her voice deadly calm, "we could extend a counter-offer. I understand that instituting a senate is a demand you cannot agree to, but might you consider offering something they would find more valuable than the death of my son?"

Elias shook his head and waved a hand. "We must scorn this kind of negotiation, or they'll be grabbing nobles' children out of the canals every day for the rest of my reign."

I wanted to throttle the skub in his chair.

Alexander gripped my hand until his nails dug just slightly into my skin. "Hold it together," he whispered.

He was right. But I didn't have to be happy about it.

I studied Elias. He seemed small sitting in front of the giant throne on which Stephanos had ruled so decisively. I wondered if he felt insecure at the prospect of filling his father's throne. For all Stephanos's faults, he'd loomed larger than life in the city since long before I was born.

"I'm not surprised by your refusal, Your Highness," said Mother, "but I must confess myself shocked by the callous manner in which you deliver it. May I remind you that my family faithfully served your father for decades? It would be becoming of you to repay that kindness by attempting to come up with a solution to bring home my son."

Elias waved his hand. "Your family did your duty to the

king, nothing more. I'm sorry about the boy, and I hope the inspectors find him soon. You are dismissed."

I caught sight of Barnabas lurking on the far side of Elias. He cast my mother a simpering smile, and I wondered whether he was behind the crown prince's newfound backbone. I'd never liked Barnabas. Neither had Mother.

Mother dipped her head. "Very well. We'll go."

I couldn't control the incredulous expression on my face as I looked from Mother to the crown prince and back. Mother, on the other hand, seemed calm and collected when she turned around. Had she known all along that Elias would give us this reception?

She snapped her fingers at Alexander and me, and we bowed in the direction of the crown prince and then followed her out of the room. As I swam away, I shot a look back at Theo. He hadn't been far ahead of me in school, and we'd always had a good rapport. "Please, help," I mouthed.

He held my gaze with a neutral expression on his face but didn't respond with a word or gesture.

⌒

"What was that about?" I whirled on Mother as soon as we left court.

She waved me off. "We won't get any help there. It was useless."

"What . . . happened? Elias seemed . . . different. I've never seen him hold his own before."

"Barnabas. The skub thinks he can use this crisis to supplant me. And maybe he's right." Barely contained rage burned in her voice, and she flicked her fin to begin swimming through the palace courtyard and toward the canal. "If my position were the only thing at stake, he wouldn't stand a chance, but my career is not our priority. First, we must get Benjamin back safely. Second, we must prevent the Neptunians from overtaking the city and destroying us all."

That's right. The Neptunians.

Alexander and I followed Mother, swimming quickly to catch up.

The Neptunian threat had been looming over us ever since they'd invaded Marbella, but in the wake of the king's assassination and Benjamin's abduction, the Neptunians had seemed distant and murky. Even though I'd seen them myself, it was easy to forget that they could arrive at any moment.

But that was only if they were coming right away. More likely, they'd take time to secure control of Marbella before turning their attention to Thessalonike.

At least I hoped so.

"So, what's your plan?" I asked when we were once again swimming side by side with her.

She reached out and grasped both my hands in hers. "You and Alexander need to go home. I have an idea for negotiating with the anti-monarchists, but I need to go alone."

"No." I shook my head. "They'll kill you. Like they killed Father."

"Maybe. But maybe I can get them to release Benjamin."

No. Not Mother, too.

I threw my arms around her. "Mother, please let me come with you. Or at least take a guard."

Visions of Mother and Benjamin dead whirlpooled in my mind. I could lose them both if she went to negotiate on her own.

She returned my embrace and then pulled back, her eyes uncharacteristically gentle as they searched mine. "I have every intention of coming home, Jade. But if I have to die, I can think of no greater cause than the safety of my children."

We'd reached the canal now, and I looked back and forth to make sure no one was near enough to overhear us. But as before, the canal was deserted. "Are you going to betray Elias?" I murmured.

The question hovered in the water between us like a shark. She turned her head away. "It's best if you don't know the details."

Elias certainly hadn't earned her loyalty, and his father had seen fit to betray us all. But Mother wasn't a traitor. Not at her core. This decision would gnaw at her for the rest of her life.

But if Benjamin died, and she felt like she could have prevented it . . . that would destroy her.

"Okay," I whispered. "But tell me where you're going. I'll send the Guard after you if you're not back in two hours."

She tilted her head. "Do you think I'll be any safer with the Guard, given what I'm about to do?"

No. Not if they knew. But she was Cleo, advisor to King Stephanos. One of the most powerful mermaids in the city. She'd be able to talk her way out of an unfriendly current with the Guard a whole lot more easily than among the anti-monarchists. So I said, "Safe? No. Safer? Undoubtedly."

She squeezed my hands more tightly. "In case it goes badly, being your mother—seeing you and your brother grow up into brave, compassionate, determined mer—has been the greatest privilege of my life."

I swallowed the lump in my throat. "You'll come home soon. With Benjamin. And everything will be alright."

She planted a kiss on the top of my head and turned toward Alexander. "You're a good match for my daughter. You always have been. And I know you'll take care of each other, no matter what."

"Mother," I choked on my words.

She placed a finger on my lips. "I'll be home as soon as I can."

I tried to memorize the way she looked—her brown eyes, gentle but determined, the way her blue hair waved just below her shoulders, the firm tilt of her mouth. But most of all, I noticed the set of her shoulders and the way she carried herself—the strength and dignity she exuded.

She wasn't afraid. She was going to save my brother, even if it cost her life.

FOUR

As soon as Mother disappeared around the corner, I collapsed against Alexander's chest, my whole body trembling.

"Shhh." He pressed a kiss to my forehead. "You've had a shock. More than one. She'll be okay."

I pulled back. "We don't know that. We don't know anything."

He rested his hands on the tops of my shoulders. "She. Will. Come. Home. We have to believe that until we're presented with clear evidence to the contrary."

I nodded, trying to will myself to believe him. But it wasn't in my nature to be optimistic, and so many things had gone wrong that I was struggling to keep hope alive. With my heart pounding wildly, I let Alexander take my hand and lead me through the canals back toward Aunt Junia's house. I tried to keep track of where we were, but the homes that I'd passed so many times growing up looked foreign and distorted, as though I were seeing the depths of the city's ugliness for the first time.

I wondered if this was how the naiads had always felt about Thessalonike. I couldn't say I blamed them.

I didn't want to hate. But I could feel an insidious anger flowing through my veins, penetrating to the core of my being. I did hate them. I hated all of them. The brutal, violent anti-monarchists who didn't care how many people they hurt in their pursuit of power. The selfish, entitled royals who threw loyalty to the depths.

With his careless, cavalier attitude, Elias had made an enemy of Mother—one of the crown's most devoted supporters. If he'd had any regard for my brother's safety, if he'd even tried to *pretend* that he was rendering some sort of aid, she would have stayed at his side as an advisor regardless of the outcome.

But he'd driven her to treason.

I wished the Neptunians would come with their army. I'd hand the whole city over to them if I had the power. Whoever they were, how could they be worse than the factions of skubs currently vying for control?

Part of me flinched back from the monstrous, revolting thoughts, but most of me was just too tired and too angry to care.

I blinked. We were outside Aunt Junia's door. Alexander turned toward me and tilted his head. "Hey. Your father wouldn't want you to think like that."

I raised my eyebrows. "Like what?"

"Don't play that game. I know you. I can read enough of what's going on inside your head."

I couldn't deny it, so I swept past him and rapped on the door. After a few moments, one of the soldiers opened it, and I swam inside. The other soldier had returned, but I saw no sign of the boy who had delivered the message.

I wondered what Mother would deliver to the anti-monarchists in exchange for Benjamin. Information? A promise to swing enough of the nobles to their side in the coup? Whatever it was, I hoped she knew what she was doing.

But now that we were with members of the Guard, we couldn't speak about anything that had happened. They still reported to the crown prince.

The taller guard tilted his head, as if asking how it had gone.

I flashed him what I hoped was a convincing smile, trusting that he'd chalk any weakness up to the horror of my brother's abduction. "Crown Prince Elias and the inspectors are doing everything they can, and we think they'll be able to bring him home soon."

I glanced down at the spot where George's body had lain the day before. I bit the inside of my cheek as the searing sting of loss pierced my chest again.

I'd lost another father.

"Where's my aunt?" I asked.

"Lying down. She had a restless night and needed to sleep."

Sleep. All at once, I realized how exhausted I was. I hadn't had a full night's sleep since leaving Marbella—I'd managed half a night with the aid of Aunt Junia's tincture—and I'd pushed myself so hard, through so much trauma, since.

But I wasn't sleepy. Just the kind of bone tired that leaves one empty but restless.

Alexander nudged me. "You should try to get some sleep, too."

I almost laughed through the hollowness in my chest. "It's not even fully dark yet. Besides, how can I?"

He grasped my arm and led me down the corridor to the room I'd slept in the night before. "Because you'll collapse if you don't."

He pulled aside the privacy screen and gestured toward the hammock. "Sleep."

I hesitated, clinging to his hand for a moment. "What about you? You must be just as tired as me."

He shook his head. "I'm not nearly as tired as you. Yes, it's been a long, hard few days, but you're reckoning with so much more." He caressed my cheek. "I'll sleep, too, love, in the front room like before. Just to be an extra set of eyes and ears."

I felt a surge of warmth and tucked myself back into his

embrace. I longed to stay there, letting him hold me through the night. But, even his closeness couldn't banish the fears that swarmed in my heart, pushing everything away except cold, numb dread. I pushed gently away from him. Weariness enveloped me. I needed to be alone, to stop fighting to keep up a brave face.

"Okay," I whispered.

He turned and swam down the hall, and I moved toward the sleeping hammock. He was right. I needed to sleep. I needed to have all my wits about me, just in case.

With an unyielding ache in my chest, I sank down in the hammock and curled up like an urchin, wrapping my arms around my fin.

Father and George, gone. Benjamin and Mother, missing. And Aunt Junia ill, nearly in shock. My family was shattered. And I couldn't think of anything to do about it.

∾

I woke from a troubled sleep just as the first light of dawn pierced my window. I'd tossed and turned for a long time, but at least I'd slept until morning. With a shake of my head, I tried to dismiss the remnants of the nightmares that had chased me through the night. I ran a hand through my hair and drifted out of my room and down the hallway to the front room.

Alexander was asleep, curled up in a hammock chair, and two new guards, a mermaid and a merman, were stationed near the door. I gave them a quick nod. "Have you heard anything?"

The mermaid, a short but powerful fighter I knew from school, shook her head. "Nothing on Benjamin. I'm sorry, Jade."

"Okay," I whispered.

"Maximus is back, though," she offered. "Orua came by to let you know that Octavian escaped on the reef and was nowhere to be found when Maximus returned for him."

I ran my hand over my face. Another thing to worry about. Octavian had tried to kill me—twice—and I hoped he hadn't made his way back to Thessalonike.

"Thank you for telling me," I said. "Is Maximus back on duty with the rest of the Guard? I'd like to bring him my condolences about his . . . brother." My voice cracked on the word brother.

The merman shook his head. "He's officially on rest from his duties. I believe he's at home."

I nodded. It made sense. Maximus lived with his mother in a small house not far from the palace. I'd paid them a visit with Tor shortly after the engagement. It seemed like a lifetime ago.

I needed to get away from prying eyes and sympathetic expressions. Before everything in me flew apart in every direction.

"I'm going to check on my aunt." I swam back down the corridor to Aunt Junia's room with even, steady strokes. One, two, three. I counted to try to keep myself calm.

Even though Aunt Junia had always lived alone, the house somehow felt strangely empty. She stirred when I peeked through the privacy screen into her chamber. "Aunt Junia?" I whispered.

She sat up and blinked at me, and a sad smile came over her face. "Oh, child. Any news?"

My throat felt hot and tight. I couldn't tell her what Mother had done. As Mother had said, the less we all knew, the better. "There was a ransom note. The crown prince can't deliver on the ransom, but everyone's trying to bring him home."

"And your mother?"

"She's out with them, of course. Working on a solution." Aunt Junia reached toward me, and I swam to her side. "And what are you doing?" she asked.

I paused. "Trying to stay out of the way, I guess. For once in my life. Trying to not make things worse."

She tsked. "That's not the Jade I know so well." Her voice gained strength and resolve with every word.

I reached for her hand. "I just don't know what to do. With the naiads, I made everything worse, and in Marbella, I was bumbling over everything. I . . . I don't know what I'm doing, and if I mess this up, he could die. A lot of people could."

She threaded her fingers through mine. "Yes, not everything you've done has worked out the way you'd hoped. But that's part of growing up. What have you learned from your earlier failures? How can you apply that to this situation?"

"By staying out of the way."

She shook her head, shifting in her hammock. "No, child. The lesson of failure isn't to flee trouble or hide from danger. It's to float above where you swam before and do a better job with the new knowledge you've earned." She studied my face. "So, what do you know?"

I closed my eyes and tried to think. My head felt fuzzy, like the stress had jumbled my thoughts into feathery red algae clumps. "I know that we're dealing with dangerous, ruthless mer. I know that if we adopt their tactics, we become just like them. That Father wouldn't want that." I clutched at the dolphin pendant that swung around my neck. "But I also know that naive idealism creates more problems than it solves."

"And what else?"

"I know that the city may be facing its biggest threat since the siren invasion a millennium ago. That we're too focused on infighting to do anything about it. That everything could change if the Neptunians come while we're this divided."

"And what else?"

My eyes flew open as warm, tingling energy surged through my core, down my arms, and out to the tips of my fingers. "I know how to get Benjamin back."

Aunt Junia grinned, something like hope on her face.

I released her hand. "Thank you."

She waved at me. "What are you waiting for, child? Go find him."

Leave it to Aunt Junia to encourage me to act without even knowing my plan.

I flew down the corridor and into the front room. "Alexander!" I yelled. "Alexander, wake up."

Alexander jolted upward from the hammock chair nearest the door, rubbing the sleep from his face. "What is it? What's wrong?"

I swam to him and grabbed him by the shoulders. "We need to act fast."

FIVE

Alexander blinked twice, slowly. "Okay . . . "

"I'll explain on the way." I grabbed his hand and dragged him toward the door. "We're going to bring him back."

Understanding dawned on his face, and he glanced at each of the guards and then back at me. "Let's go."

The guards glanced at each other, as if unsure whether or not they should stop us. But we weren't prisoners, and the older of the two only mumbled, "Be careful."

We slipped out of the house and down the pathway to the canal. Few mer were in sight, but in case anyone was watching, I wrapped my arm around Alexander's and drew him close, as if I were whispering something romantic in his ear. "Maximus is back. He can help."

Alexander tilted his head and gave me a look like I'd lost my mind. "How?"

I swallowed. "Because he's just lost his brother." My voice cracked. "He can convince the anti-monarchists that he's on their side. I'm sure of it. And he won't let them do to Benjamin what the king did to Andronicus."

Alexander stopped and turned me to face him. "You're putting a lot of faith in him, Jade. After he finds out about Andronicus's execution, how do you know he'll still be loyal to the monarchy?"

"I don't," I murmured. "But I think he'll be loyal to a

friend. And to tell you the truth, I'm not sure I'm loyal to the monarchy either."

Alexander fell silent, but he nodded, and we continued down the canal in the direction of the palace.

I ran my plan over and over again in my head. It wasn't a sure thing. I could think of at least four places where everything could fall apart. But I couldn't dwell on those yet. I would just take one thing at a time.

As long as the crown prince didn't know that Mother had played the rogue, we had a chance.

And as long as I could convince Maximus to help me. And Maximus could convince the anti-monarchists that Andronicus's death had entirely upended his loyalty to the crown. And Maximus was able to find and release Benjamin.

Nerves curled in my stomach. This wasn't my very worst idea—in fact, I really thought it might work—but I'd be asking Maximus to risk his life for Benjamin. It was a lot to ask of anyone, and while Maximus and I had developed deep respect for each other, it wasn't like we had a long history. Two months earlier, he'd thought me a vicious liar.

But we'd cross that drop-off when we came to it.

When we'd nearly reached the soaring coral of the palace's spires, we turned abruptly right, down a side street lined by modest houses owned mostly by members of the Guard who weren't of noble birth. I looked from side to side at the tidy homes and tried to remember which one Tor and I had visited.

"That one," I said finally, squinting at a dark blue house with teal fan coral around the windows. The memory solidified in my mind, and nostalgia tugged at my throat. Tor and I had been so happy then. I'd been thrilled to marry him.

I stole a glance at Alexander. I wouldn't trade what we had for anything in the world, but I wished with everything in me that my relationship with Tor hadn't been dashed up on the rocks so spectacularly. That, somehow, we'd both quietly realized that we didn't want to get married and ended things at peace with each other. That he hadn't killed someone and forced me to turn him in. That together we hadn't unleashed so much horror on the city.

Maybe everything would have been different if I'd reconnected with Alexander before Tor started vying for my attention.

But I couldn't turn back time, and I'd get caught in a whirlpool I couldn't escape if I let my thoughts circle on all the ways things could have turned out differently.

We drew close to the door, and I knocked softly.

A middle-aged mermaid dressed in black answered the door. Maximus's mother. Mariana, I thought her name was, but I didn't remember for sure.

"Is-is Maximus here?" I asked.

"Jade?" Maximus asked from the other side of the room. His mother didn't say a word, but turned and swam into another room, out of sight.

Maximus took her place in the doorway. "I'm sorry," he said, glancing back at the room his mother had disappeared into. "This really isn't a good time. I-my brother died while we were in Marbella."

I searched his face and saw the signs of grief heavy on his countenance. Guilt turned my stomach. It felt wrong to ask him to save my brother when he'd just learned that he'd lost his. It felt worse to endanger Mariana's last living child.

But I wasn't going to let guilt get in the way of saving Benjamin. There would be plenty of time to search my conscience and agonize later.

"I'm so sorry." I rubbed the back of my neck. "I heard. I-I wish I was here to bring you a mourning gift."

He stared at me, waiting for me to continue.

"I need your help," I finally said.

Maximus's jaw tightened, and he glanced from me to

Alexander. "And of all the mer in the city, you're coming to me right now because . . . "

Alexander rested his hands on my shoulders. "Jade's brother has been taken by the anti-monarchists. They're threatening to kill him, to drop him live into the depths."

Maximus gripped the doorframe until his knuckles turned white. "They did?"

"It's a ransom," I said. "They're trying to get the crown prince to install a senate, but it's useless. The monarchy . . . knows no loyalty except to itself."

Maximus ran a hand over his face. "So I've heard." He paused. "How can I help?"

I closed my eyes. "I hate to ask this of you, but we didn't know of anyone else who might be able to gain their trust quickly."

He chewed on his lower lip. "You want me to use my brother's death to convince them that I've turned?"

When he phrased it that way, it sounded awful. Worse than awful. But Benjamin's face loomed in my mind, and I plunged forward. "Yes." I held his gaze. "I know it's a lot to ask, especially right now, but I don't know how else to save Benjamin."

"No." He shook his head. "It's not a lot to ask. I, of all people, know what it's like to lose a brother." He glanced backward into the house and then swam forward and closed the door. "I don't want my mother to hear our conversation. She's lost too much recently."

Discomfort churned in my stomach. I didn't want the anti-monarchists to overhear our conversation either. Or to see us together.

Maximus seemed to sense my hesitation. "We're just going there." He gestured to a door set in a nondescript sand-stone building across the canal.

I raised an eyebrow in silent question, but we followed him across the canal and to the mysterious door. Maximus tapped on the door three times before opening it and letting himself in. With a glance at Alexander and a shrug, I followed, Alexander at my side.

I blinked against the darkness. The door had opened into a long corridor.

I almost laughed. Was Maximus taking us to somewhere isolated to kill us?

The notion was absurd, of course, but I couldn't suppress the tingle that ran down my spine.

"Don't worry." Maximus looked back at us, and I could just barely make out his features in the dim light. "This isn't where we torture dissidents."

I wasn't sure if he was joking or not.

We followed him through a right turn into a bare room. This one was better lit. Though it didn't have a window, enough bioluminaries covered the ceiling to cast the room in a gentle glow. I took in the six hammock chairs around a low stone table and moved to sit down.

This was some sort of meeting place, then, for the Guard.

Alexander pulled a chair out next to me, and we sank down into our seats.

Maximus sat across from us, and I studied his face again. The sadness I'd seen there when we first arrived at his door had dissipated, and intense focus had taken its place.

"You're sure about this?" I asked.

He waved his hand. "It gives me something to focus on. Tell me what happened."

With a little shudder, I recounted everything that had happened since he'd left to retrieve Octavian.

When I got to the Crown Prince Elias's reaction to the ransom note, he nearly lurched up from his seat. "He said what?"

I offered a shrug.

Maximus slammed his fist on the table, and rage danced in his eyes.

If the crown prince isn't careful, Maximus won't just

pretend to join the anti-monarchists. But I shook away the thought. No matter how badly the royals behaved, the anti-monarchists weren't a good alternative. Surely, Maximus knew that.

How do you choose between two corrupt factions?

Maybe we didn't choose. Maybe we just had to do our best to tread water in the torrent that raged around us. But that wasn't a tenable choice forever. Eventually we'd find ourselves slammed up against the rocks.

So maybe we had to swim deeper.

I bit my lip. The metaphor could only stretch so far before it snapped.

When Maximus composed himself, I continued the story, not even omitting my conversation with Mother and her decision to go to try to bargain.

Concern shadowed his expression. "Have you heard from her since?"

I shook my head. "She left yesterday afternoon. I hope . . . I hope they're just using her as another bargaining shell. But I have to face the reality that Benjamin's fate may rest with me now."

"With us." Alexander squeezed my hand, and I'd never been so grateful for him.

"With us."

Maximus stared up at the ceiling. "With all of us," he murmured.

Hope flared in my chest. We were stronger together.

After a moment, Maximus trained his gaze on me again. "Is there anything else you can remember? Whether it seems relevant or not."

I thought about it but shook my head. "No. I've told you everything."

He drummed his fingers on the table. "We don't have any time to lose. I'll go now." He hesitated. "Find Orua. Tell her what's going on. And tell her I love her."

I dipped my head. "Of course." It was the least we could do.

"I'll send a message when I know anything more," he said. "Where will you be staying?"

"At my aunt's house. Junia Ariapola. On Mangrove Canal."

He nodded and met my gaze again, as if wanting to say something else, but then he dropped his gaze and pushed up from the table. "Go there now. I'll leave out the back and find my brother's friends."

As we turned and left Maximus behind, I wondered if we'd ever see him again.

CHAPTER

SIX

"Let's go see Orua first," I murmured as we eased onto the empty canal. Even the larger canals were still all but deserted since the assassination. Mer didn't want to leave the safety of their homes in the face of such uncertainty.

I assumed that the guards wouldn't change shift for several hours, at least, and I didn't want to wait to bring Maximus's message to Orua.

"Do you know where she lives?" asked Alexander.

I closed my eyes and tried to think. "No. I only ever saw her in Lavinia's offices. I can think of a few mer who would know." Maximus's mother particularly. "But I don't want anyone to start asking too many questions."

We hovered in silence, staring at each other. Alexander reached out and grabbed my hands. I started to pull back, relieved to realize that my wrist wasn't sore anymore, but he didn't let go. "Let's not look too serious, love. We don't want to draw attention."

He drew me into an embrace and whispered, "You and Orua just returned from a long journey. I don't think it will raise too many questions if we ask around to try to find her. There are a thousand pretexts we could use."

I tried to relax, but the tension weighed so heavily it seemed to be driving me down toward the seafloor. My brow twitched.

"Hey." He gazed into my eyes. "Stay focused. We'll get through this."

"I know." I set my jaw. "How did the naiads do it for so long, Alexander? How did they survive with so much uncertainty? I've had a really bad . . . what, two months? Three? And I'm falling apart. I don't know how to navigate any of this. And they had to deal with it day in and day out for years at a time with no sign of abatement." I stared past his shoulder at a stand of waving coral. "I used to wonder why the liberationists were so popular in the months leading up to Father's death, but now I realize how amazing it is that so few of the naiads turned to the liberationist movement."

"Jade, it's—"

"Never mind. Let's just find Orua." My shoulders tensed. "We'll start with Maximus's mother. We can say he was called away on Guard business and that he's asked us to pass a message on but that we forgot to ask him where to find her."

He shrugged. "Seems as good an excuse as any. And pretty close to the truth, as these things go."

⌒

Maximus's mother didn't know where Orua lived, and Lavinia was nowhere to be found at her office. Probably hiding out in her house like the rest of the city. My shoulders slumped as I realized we'd hit a dead end. Evening was descending on the city, and it didn't feel safe to be out and about.

An hour later, Alexander, Aunt Junia, and I sat glumly around the table, staring at each other. A'a napped in my lap, and the two guards from earlier were still stationed at the door. Now that I'd recruited Maximus's help and he too had disappeared into the fray, I again felt as if *I* were doing nothing to get Benjamin back. The tension weighed on me in relentless waves.

"George's father sent a message," Aunt Junia said. "The funeral will be tomorrow afternoon, after the rites for the king are completed."

The king's funeral already? How quickly the days were passing.

"George won't be given a court funeral, of course," said Aunt Junia.

Of course. Because he wasn't a noble. It rankled me.

"They're going to hold the rite at the drop-off and cast his body to the depths." Aunt Junia picked at a piece of lobster in front of her but didn't seem to have much of an appetite.

A knock sounded at the door.

A messenger? I set A'a gently on the table and darted to the door. The guards stiffened as I reached for the handle, but they didn't interfere, and I flung the door open.

Pippa stood on the other side, and I ushered her in.

"Did you get my messages?" I asked.

"Yes." She closed the door behind her and took special care to latch it securely. "I tried to come earlier, but it wasn't safe in the canals. Have they found him yet?"

I shook my head. "We're doing everything we can, and it still feels so woefully inadequate." My voice shook. "I just keep thinking of him, trapped and scared."

Pippa wrapped her arms around me. "I understand, dear."

I chewed my lip. Her own sister's death must still be fresh for her.

"Hey!" Aunt Junia's startled voice broke the moment of shared grief. I whirled around. A'a had darted across the table and taken a bite out of Aunt Junia's lobster.

"A'a!" I swam over and scooped him up, scolding him and placing him on a hammock chair.

Pippa leaned against the table, her eyes fixed on A'a as

she spoke. "Maybe you should try to do something about it. About Benjamin."

I squinted at her. She'd chastised me for rushing head-long into danger as if I controlled the whole ocean, and now she was pushing me to act rashly?

A wry expression overtook her face. "Don't look at me like that. I'm not suggesting you behave like an idiot."

I crossed my arms. "I never act like an idiot."

Pippa and Alexander both burst out laughing, and I scowled at them. "Fine."

It felt good to be lighthearted for just a moment. We needed to laugh, I suspected, or we'd curl up like sea urchins at the horror of it all.

But I didn't let myself think that things couldn't get any worse. I'd thought that before, and we were plumbing new depths.

The somber thoughts erased my momentary smile. "What else can I do? I've thought so hard, but I'm completely out of ideas."

"Would Theo be able to help us?" Alexander asked. "You got along with him in school."

I thought back to the sympathetic look Theo had given me as we left court. He hadn't defended us then, but maybe we could persuade him. Or perhaps Tor could help us. I hated the thought of asking him, but he had saved my life when the webbed-foot dragon attacked our envoy to Marbella. But then again, did Tor have connections anymore?

And what if Maximus sends a message while I'm gone?

I groaned. The stakes were too high for uncertainty.

A scream shattered the quiet, and I flew to the window and peered through the narrow crack between the bolted shutters. I couldn't see anything. "Depths," I hissed.

Something in me suspected it was a trap, that we were being lured to open the door.

"Pippa, take Aunt Junia to the back of the house. Hide

as best as you can, but be prepared to flee out the back if need be."

Pippa tightened her jaw but nodded and rested her hand on Aunt Junia's arm.

Aunt Junia harrumphed. "I hardly think—"

I held up my hand, the beginnings of a plan percolating in my head. If the commotion outside was a coincidence, it would all come to nothing, of course.

Muffled shouts sounded outside our door, and Aunt Junia followed Pippa down the corridor and out of sight.

I made eye contact with the guards, and the mermaid nodded abruptly. "Stay back," she cautioned. "We'll check it out first."

Reasonable.

As the two guards exited the house, I backed away from the door, half expecting a blood-hungry mob to burst in.

But instead, Ti swam in, flanked by the guards.

I squinted at her, confused, and she gave me a wry smile.

"A harpy in the canals is a terrifying sight," she said in a deadpan tone.

I rushed forward and threw my arms around her, and after a slight hesitation, she returned my hug. "I have news of your brother."

My heart pounded in my ears. "Where is he? Is he alright?"

"I don't know where he is, exactly, but the new leader of the anti-monarchists—Faustus, his name is—assured me no harm had come to him."

"And Mother? Did they say anything of her?"

Ti tilted her head. "Your mother? What about her?"

With a glance at the guards, I ushered Ti down the hall. "Pippa! Aunt Junia! It's safe."

In response, A'a skittered out of Aunt Junia's room and paddled toward me. I scooped him up and set him on my shoulder, and as he snuggled into my neck, I felt a little part of myself relax. Something was right with the world, even if everything else was shattered.

"We're in here," Pippa called from Aunt Junia's room, but I ushered Ti into the chamber that Benjamin had been staying in, further down the corridor, all the way to the back of the house.

When I was sure the guards hadn't followed us, I faced Ti. "Mother went to the anti-monarchists to try to bargain with them directly. We haven't heard from her since."

Ti pursed her lips. "Well, if Faustus knew of Cleo's whereabouts, he didn't let on to me. But that doesn't mean they don't have her, of course."

"Wait . . . you spoke to them directly?" I drew back in surprise.

"I did," said Ti. "The horrid mer requested a meeting, and I thought it prudent to comply. They're interested in details of Marbella's government. In how democracy works, at its core. I gave them some information but then said that democracy didn't work if the citizenry weren't equals, and that every truly democratic society I'd heard of had to let go of its backward prejudices to survive. Mob rule that doesn't respect the rights of every citizen only turns the tides red."

My jaw dropped. It shouldn't have surprised me that Ti had spoken boldly, but I wouldn't have expected her to speak quite *that* boldly.

"As you might have guessed, that didn't go over well. I also told them that bloodshed only attracted sharks, and they didn't love that either." She dragged a clawed hand through her hair. "There's a reason I'm a senator, not a diplomat."

"And what about Benjamin?" I clasped both my hands behind my neck.

"Faustus was willing to confirm that he was safe but, naturally, not where he was being held. He seemed to be holding out hope that Elias might commission a senate." She shook her head. "He's either a fool, or he's trying to trick all of us. I hope it's the latter. We also talked about what it would mean if the Neptunians showed up in the middle of his coup attempt."

I blinked twice. *So the anti-monarchists have been fully informed of that threat.*

Ti scoffed. "He seemed to welcome them. He expressed hope that they would come and he could strike a bargain to retain local control—through a senate, of course, once the crown prince was unseated—and pay tribute. He really believed that pledging fealty to a distant power was better than submitting to the authority of a local king."

"Maybe he's right," I murmured.

A sharp look crossed Ti's face. "Give no quarter to killers and thieves, Miss Cleopola. I don't care how many political ideals I share with them. I've always believed it better to lose an election than my honor."

"I don't sympathize with them," I retorted. "But I'd be lying if I said the idea that Neptunian rule might be better than local rule had never crossed my mind."

Ti's eyes softened. "You don't know of what you speak, Miss Cleopola."

I bit my lip. Part of me knew I was being naive, but we were out of good options, and I was grasping for purchase in an ever-faster current. "I'm sorry."

She eased herself into a seated position on the sleeping hammock, and I sank to the floor. "You're giving in to despair, but you need to snap yourself out of it. These are hard days, and there may be even harder ones ahead, but if we let cynicism deaden us into complacency or inaction . . . well then, we've already lost."

"So, what do we do?" Even as I asked, I a surge of longing swept over me—to be strong and decisive like Ti.

"We hold firm to our beliefs, and we prepare ourselves to act on them whenever the opportunity presents itself. And if no opportunity is forthcoming, we make one."

CHAPTER

SEVEN

A tablet came from Maximus that night.

After I tipped the messenger, I beckoned Alexander and Pippa, and we swam to the kitchen, away from the eyes of the Guard. Ti and Aunt Junia were already sitting at the table, picking at a salad. I tore open the wrapping on the tablet.

B is safe for now, it read.

Relief flooded my chest, and my gills relaxed. The confirmation of Ti's report soothed my worried thoughts. I continued reading.

I've inserted myself among them as someone who is on their side but wants the situation to resolve peacefully—to be honest, I don't know that it's far from the truth these days. I'm not in their leader's inner circle, but he's keeping me close to try to get information from me. I believe B is being kept within the city. I haven't yet learned of C's whereabouts. I'll send word when I know more.

It was unsigned, but I had no doubts as to its authorship.

Benjamin was safe and inside the city, but still no word of Mother.

Did she even make it to the anti-monarchists? Or did the crown prince somehow learn of her plans first?

The voice of the crier sounded from the canals, but he wasn't near Aunt Junia's house yet, and I couldn't quite make out his words. At least not from the back of the house.

"What does it say?" Alexander nudged my shoulder.

Aunt Junia and Pippa were also looking at me expectantly.

"Benjamin's still alive," I said, my voice hoarse. "We still don't know anything about Mother, good or bad."

Aunt Junia closed her eyes, and I wondered whether she was having the same doubts I was.

"But it seems like Maximus is making progress," I continued. "Hopefully we'll get more news soon."

As if on cue, the crier's voice sounded again, louder this time. He must have turned onto our canal. I still couldn't make out every word, but I got the gist: Elias's coronation date had been set for five days hence.

Unease churned in my stomach. I hadn't always paid perfect attention in school, but I did remember that there was customarily a one-month mourning period between the death of the monarch and the coronation of the heir.

Elias was moving quickly, I supposed because tensions were running so high. But I wondered if a break in tradition would only enrage the anti-monarchists further—perhaps giving them a pretext for action.

And after all, if a minor tradition could be so easily discarded, what about major ones?

Alexander stared at the shutter. "The coronation shouldn't happen for weeks."

I ran my hands through my hair. If the anti-monarchists saw this as an act of aggression, I could only hope our loved ones wouldn't get caught in the ensuing maelstrom.

Benjamin. Mother. Maximus. Too many people I cared about were in their net.

Perhaps Theo could be reasoned with.

"Ti," I said, "will you come with me to court, tomorrow after George's funeral? I think it's time we had a long conversation with the younger prince."

Ti dipped her head. "He does seem like the more

reasonable of the two, doesn't he? It's a pity the succession is so constrained."

I couldn't put my finger on why exactly I thought Theo might be willing to help us. *Maybe it's nothing more than wishful thinking on my part.* But like Ti had said, if opportunities didn't present themselves, we had to create our own tides.

And we needed to do it before more mer ended up dead.

King Stephanos's funeral was a predictably stagnant affair, with the Liturgy of Loss sung entirely in an ancient language, rather than spoken by the people as was customary. We arrived late and left as soon as it ended, not accompanying the procession to the drop-off, to make Mother's absence less conspicuous.

She'd be sad she'd missed the funeral. Even though she'd grown angry at Stephanos's erratic decisions in his last months, she'd been one of his closest advisors for many years.

After the funeral, we rushed home to see if Orua was back on duty at Aunt Junia's house, and relief filled me when she answered the door.

"Can I talk to you? In the back?" I asked. "I need to . . . work through something that happened in Marbella."

She regarded me with a suspicious gaze, but the soldier on duty alongside her didn't seem to notice.

I swam behind her to the kitchen.

When we reached the table, she sat in one of the hammock chairs and eyed me. "What's this really about?" she asked, keeping her voice quiet.

"I don't have much time. I'm leaving for another funeral soon. But Maximus is infiltrating the anti-monarchists to try to help get Benjamin and my mother back."

"Your mother?"

I held up a hand. "They have her, too. Please don't tell anyone."

"And Max . . . why?" she hissed.

I gripped the edge of the table. "Please don't hate me. I asked him. They'll believe him because the king just killed Andronicus."

Rage churned in her eyes. "They *might* believe him. And what if the crown prince gets word of it?"

"I know it's a risk," I said. "And so does he. Though of course I'll vouch for him with Elias if that becomes an issue. Listen, he wanted me to tell you that he loves you."

Her eyes softened. "I don't hate you, Jade. But it might take me some time to forgive this. He just lost his brother. He's grieving."

"And I might be about to lose mine!" I said too loudly. She glanced at the corridor, and I fell silent.

"I know," she said. "That's why I don't hate you." She pushed up from the table. "I should be in the front room."

"Orua, wait!"

She shook her head without turning around to look back at me. "Don't you have a funeral to get to?"

I looked over at the tide glass. She was right. We should go soon. The mourners for the king would be leaving the drop-off right about now.

I let Orua go without saying anything else, and Alexander, Pippa, and I left the house together quietly, swimming toward the city gates at a brisk pace. We passed the soldiers at the entrance to the city without speaking and made our way to the edge of the reef for George's funeral.

About ten other mer were there. I recognized George's father, Cado, an elderly mer with piercing black eyes. "Lady Jade," he said in a creaky, aged voice. "Thank you so much for coming." He looked at each of us in turn, and in a voice equal parts hurt and confusion, he said, "Are your mother and brother not attending?"

I reached out and took his hands. "They would be here if they could," I said. "They're being held captive by George's murderers. We're . . . doing everything we can to bring them back, and to bring those responsible to justice."

He drew back. "I'm so sorry. I didn't know." He cast a hard look toward the city. "I hope the skubs pay dearly."

"Me too," I said, unsure what else to say. I looked past the crowd to see a body wrapped in kelp at the edge of the drop-off. George.

I felt numb.

The magistrate swept toward us over the reef and hovered over George's body. "Are we ready to begin?" she asked in a solemn voice.

"Yes," came a handful of voices from the gathered mer.

"Would anyone like to say a few words about Georgios?" she asked.

Cado raised his hand, swam to the front, and turned toward us. He picked at a thread that had come loose on his wrap. "George was a devoted son," he said. "He always made sure his mother and I were taken care of, and he was even more regular with his visits after her passing. He knew what was important in life. I'm not given to many words, but . . . " He looked down at George's body, and his voice quavered. "Dark are the tides that take the son before the father."

A lump rose in my throat.

"He was a good merman," he continued. "I was proud to have raised him. And I'll miss him dearly." He opened his mouth as if he wanted to say more, but then he shook his head and swam back into the crowd.

"Anyone else?" called the magistrate as she straightened her wrap.

I released Alexander's hand and found myself moving toward the front of the crowd. When I reached George's body,

I turned to look back at everyone. Alexander gave me an encouraging smile.

"George was like a second father to me," I began, my voice squeaking at first but gaining strength with each word. "I've known him since I was a little girl, and when my own father died, George became the only father I still had. He was quick to speak words of love and wisdom into my life, and his death leaves a hole in our family that no one else can fill. We'll all miss his sense of humor and practical jokes." My gills flared. "And I was so lucky to have him in my life. Thank you all for sharing him with us."

I glided back through the crowd to Alexander and Pippa, feeling the crushing weight of George's loss throbbing in my chest.

George's niece spoke next, but I didn't hear anything she said.

Then the magistrate returned to the front to begin the Liturgy of Loss. "We mourn the loss of Georgios Cadopolos and rail against the whims of the tides."

"For the tides have taken him," we intoned.

"As the tides will take us all," she called.

"Let us remember we will die." I gazed out over the deep water, thinking of those we'd lost to its depths. Father's body was down there, somewhere. Yvonna. Most recently, the king.

"Search your heart; search your life."

I murmured the response by rote.

The dirge wasn't sung—I supposed because we didn't have the court cantor—instead we chanted it. Though I didn't know ancient Phoenan, the language of the dirge, I knew the song well enough.

As the dirge ended, the magistrate spoke the final chant. "We demand justice."

I glanced up, startled. This part of the funeral liturgy was only used in cases of murder, and yet it had become so familiar. *The last three funerals I've attended have all been for murder victims.*

"Let us commend Georgios's body to the care of the depths," said the magistrate.

We formed a line and, one by one, swam past George's body. Some reached out to touch him as they passed by. George's father knelt beside him for a moment. I leaned over and kissed his kelp-wrapped forehead.

After the line of guests had paid their respects, two of George's family members moved forward to pick up the body, which was weighted down by rocks.

I hid my face behind Alexander's shoulder when they threw George into the abyss.

CHAPTER

EIGHT

G rief still heavy on my heart, I entered the magnificent court hesitantly, but Ti's imposing presence overshadowed my insecurities.

"We'd like an audience with Prince Theo," Ti announced to the guards at the door.

They glanced at us and shrugged. "He's in there. I suppose you can go in."

We glided past them and into the imposing hall. Elias, Theo, and two advisors—Barnabas included, I noted with a suppressed growl—were gathered at the front of the room just underneath the empty throne, and a troop of the Guard was stationed on either side of them.

My jaw nearly dropped when I saw an artist off to our right beginning a sketch on one of the empty wall panels. I could only hope it was to commemorate King Stephanos and not Crown Prince Elias's ascent to power. But the art in this room was reserved for the most significant events in our culture's history. That a new panel was being carved now struck me as wrong, somehow.

We drew near, and while a few of the soldiers tightened their grips on their weapons as they looked at Ti, most of them ignored us.

"Prince Theo?" I ventured when we were within easy earshot.

Here it was. The last thing that I could possibly imagine might make any difference.

Theo glanced up at us, and the stony expression on his face softened. "Jade. Senator."

Ti bowed. "We've come to ask your advice on an important matter."

I fought to keep a neutral expression on my face and ignore the rumpled look Crown Prince Elias gave to the advisors and to Theo. But he didn't move to intervene as Theo handed the tablet he was holding to Advisor Galena and swam to us.

"The problem is of a sensitive nature," said Ti. "I'd rather the guards didn't overhear us, and it seems imprudent to ask them to leave the crown prince's side. Perhaps we could seek out a more private place?"

Now Crown Prince Elias really did seem alarmed. He leaned over to confer in whispers with Barnabas, though he still didn't interfere.

"Of course," said Theo. "We'll go into the meeting chambers." He nodded to the rooms that lined the court to my right, and then Theo, Ti, and I floated across the room and into a small side chamber. Even here, the stone walls were wrought with imposing carvings and extravagant filigree, telling stories of the gloried history of the city. The most significant history. I glanced back at the new panel being carved just before Theo closed the door behind us.

I cocked my head as I looked at one of the carvings paneling this room—portraying a story I didn't recognize but which seemed to show a Thessaloniken monarch turning away a group of caecilias. The carven caecilias bore harsh features and sharp teeth, and the final panel showed a safe, happy crowd of mer, celebrating the rejection of the interlopers.

A sick feeling turned in my gut as I wondered what had really happened that day. Surely, a dozen caecilias weren't a security risk to a robust city. I wondered why they'd come and how we'd sent them away. I couldn't imagine it had really been a moment to glorify. More likely a moment we ought to mourn.

I shook the thought away and turned to Theo. "Please." I searched his eyes. "We're desperate. Time's running out, and . . . " My voice caught in my throat.

Ti trained her gaze on Theo. "Your city is in crisis. Your brother seems intent on alienating his most loyal friends with his rash decisions and diplomatic clumsiness. If the threats were only internal, it'd be bad enough, but I can attest that the external threat being borne on the currents is deadlier than anything you can imagine."

Theo cracked his neck. "I'm aware of the situation, Senator. What would you have me do?"

"Your brother is not to be reasoned with?"

He shifted. "Elias chooses his own advisors. Right now, he's listening closely to Barnabas's counsel."

I'd always thought Barnabas was a serpent.

I pushed water through my gills. "Is that why the coronation is happening so soon?"

Theo's jaw tightened. "I'm not at liberty to discuss that."

"Theo." I crossed my arms.

He closed his eyes. "Jade, don't. I'm a prince of Thessalonike. I have to act like one."

"Which means you bear responsibility for the mer. For their protection."

"Do you think that hasn't been weighing on me every moment since they killed my father?" he hissed, and the pained expression on his face softened my resolve.

But my family was in danger. So was the whole city. For all I'd said—and thought—about neither the royal family nor the anti-monarchists being good options, we really had no idea what the Neptunians might do if they invaded. Would rulers, however distant they might agree to remain, who had no love for the city or any of its occupants prove any better than our deeply imperfect local leadership?

We might not be able to stop the Neptunians, but at least we needed to try. And we wouldn't be able to stop them if we were fractured and divided.

Theo knew all of this already, surely. But if Elias wasn't taking his advice, how much could be done about it?

Ti grasped her claw-like hands. "I have a solution in mind that might resolve any number of our problems."

Theo scoffed. "Do you now?"

Ti stared at him, annoyance and compassion warring in her eyes. "Are you interested in hearing what this harpy has to say, young merman, or will you dismiss me outright?"

Theo squirmed underneath her intense gaze. "I'm sorry for sounding so dismissive, Senator. I'll listen."

Ti stretched upward and shifted her eyes toward the wall. "You need unity, and you need it fast. You have nothing to gain from a drawn-out dispute with the anti-monarchists or the Neptunians."

"I know this." A hint of irritation colored Theo's voice.

"You know it." Ti tapped the side of her head. "But have you really thought about the cost? About what will happen if the Neptunians come while the anti-monarchists are vying for power?"

"The anti-monarchists are always vying for power," said Theo.

"You know it's different right now," I interjected.

"A transition is always a particularly unstable time." Ti pressed her fingers together. "You can be forgiven for not knowing that as well as I do. In democracies like Marbella, the balance of power shifts and reshifts every year."

"Every year?" Theo's jaw dropped. "How do you ever get anything done?"

A bitter smile curled Ti's lips. "Sometimes we didn't. But

we had the goodwill of the people." She chuckled. "Well, most of the time."

Theo massaged his temples. "Tell me, Senator, what would you have me do?"

I suspected he was still fighting to mask his irritation, but he did a decent job.

"Give the people what they want. Or at least a credible peace offering."

Theo's head snapped up. "You want me to tell my brother that the senator from Marbella says to give the people a senate?"

Ti's shrewd eyes narrowed on him. "Not a senate, young one. I'm not so naive as to think that a young princeling accustomed to the idea that he will inherit absolute power will give it up so easily. No, I'm proposing a much less complete solution. One your brother might be convinced to go along with."

I looked from Ti to Theo and back again. Ti radiated the sort of deadly calm that felt simultaneously reassuring and dangerous. Theo, on the other hand, was displaying an almost frenetic range of emotions in his face and body language—fear, grief, anger, hope, disgust.

I felt for him. The same current that brought about the death of his father was threatening to upend his whole view of the world.

But I knew Theo to be a good, generous, reasonable merman. I harbored hope that he could be brought to see reason.

"Offer the people the chance to elect representatives according to their location in the city." Ti was staring at the wall now, as if still working out the finer points of the solution in her head. "This new governing body won't have the authority to overrule the king, but they can vote on non-binding resolutions to offer him their opinion, and he can give them jurisdiction over any matters he opts not to personally handle himself. Thus, the king cedes none of his power but still offers the people something of value. Some degree of self-rule."

Theo seemed to consider the idea. "Under normal circumstances, Elias might contemplate such a thing. But Barnabas has spent days now convincing him that he must respond to the people with strength. That any compromise is a sign of weakness. I'm sure that they would say that such a solution would usher in the waning of the monarchy."

"If the Neptunians arrive while we are still divided, your monarchy will not wane. It will dissolve." Ti's eyes were intense now. "My city fell, young one, because we had no warning. Your city has the benefit of advance notice. Do not squander it."

A cry from the central room of the court sent quillpricks down my spine.

"It's him," called a voice.

I flew to the doorway and gazed out at the room. A figure floating before the crown prince caught my eye.

Benjamin.

NINE

y thoughts were swirling so fast I couldn't keep up with them. But I felt the relief in all its fullness descend on me and suck every particle of energy from my body. As if some part of me had been tightly coiled around itself for days, and now that it was unwinding, I didn't know if I could hold myself together.

But then it hit me.

Mother. She saved him.

I surged toward Benjamin and tackled him from behind, enfolding him in the tightest hug I'd ever given him. "You're alive." My voice caught.

"Jade?"

I released him and then swam around to see him face-to-face. "Did they hurt you?"

He shook his head, his lips pressed together tightly. "I'm fine."

Something in his expression struck me as too old, as if he'd grown up while he was away.

"What is it?" I asked, panic rising in my chest.

"They have Mother."

I knew it, of course. I'd seen her leave myself, preparing to bargain for her son's life with the people who'd killed her husband. I'd seen the steel in her eyes and known she would do anything necessary to make sure Benjamin came home safely.

And here he was.

Barnabas blustered something behind me, and I knew everyone else had heard Benjamin's announcement.

"The anti-monarchists?" I asked, even though I didn't need to.

Benjamin nodded. "They told me to come tell the crown prince that they'd begin torturing her for information if he didn't reply to their demands today."

"Their demands?"

He proffered a tablet.

I snatched it before anyone could intervene.

"They want a senate," I said, my voice flat. "The same as in the ransom note for you, urchin."

I turned around, every muscle heavy, and faced the crown prince. "Your Highness, please. I know you won't give them a senate, but give them something."

"If I may," said Theo from my right.

I glanced at him, startled. I hadn't realized he'd followed me out of the council room. Ti was there, too, looking at Theo with a hint of a smile on her face.

Elias shrugged in Theo's direction. Barnabas looked at each of us in turn, and I couldn't read his expression. But I knew it didn't bode well.

Theo floated straight and tall, and his voice didn't waver as he spoke. "There's no reason we can't extend a sign that we want peace with them, brother."

"What do you mean?" asked Elias.

"Of course, Thessalonike must remain a monarchy, as she has always been. We must safeguard Father's legacy—our family's legacy, which goes back millennia. But that doesn't mean we must rule with fear."

Elias's eyes flicked to Ti and then back to Theo. "Don't tell me you're going soft on pro-democracy sentiment within my own court."

Theo laughed. "Listen to yourself, Elias." His eyes softened,

61

and a hint of humor lingered on his face. "You're treating me like an enemy at the gates."

Elias relaxed a little. "I'm sorry. We're all under deep-sea pressure right now."

Theo continued, "Listen to me. I'm not suggesting we concede to the anti-monarchists. We will not dismantle what our ancestors have built. But that doesn't mean we can't try to make peace with them."

Elias raised a manicured eyebrow.

"We could allow the people to elect representatives to form a governing body under your authority," said Theo. "You could allow them to operate in whatever spheres you would normally delegate to mer you appoint. Let them feel they have a partial democracy, even as you retain the final say in everything that goes on in the city."

Elias seemed to consider this.

Barnabas bowed to Elias. "Your Majesty, I must protest against this in the strongest possible terms."

I stiffened.

But Theo responded, "Elias, listen to reason. Barnabas says he has your best interests at heart, but what has his counsel led to? It's only emboldened the anti-monarchists. And regardless of what he says about needing to respond with force, we cannot afford to have our contingency plans tortured out of Cleo."

Barnabas harrumphed. "We have no reason to assume that the anti-monarchists would release Cleo in exchange for this bastardized senate your brother is proposing. And once you start compromising, they'll demand more and more until your whole rule is overthrown."

"We're all going to be overthrown!" shouted Theo, moving toward Barnabas. "Are you being paid by the Neptunians to keep us in chaos until they come and finish us off?"

"Don't be prepost—"

"Because that's what it sounds like." Theo grabbed

Barnabas by the shoulders and drew his face in close. "I think you're bent on undermining the monarchy, and you're giving advice you know will devastate us all."

Barnabas jerked backward and straightened his wrap. He turned to Elias with a sulky expression on his face. "Your Highness, you can see how abominably I was just treated."

I studied Elias's face, trying to read the layers of emotion that rested just under the surface. I didn't think he believed Theo's allegation that Barnabas was a traitor—I don't think any of us did, though I knew Barnabas was a conniving little shark—but the performance seemed to sway Elias.

Elias stared straight at Theo. "You will not mistreat my advisors in such a way." But then his face relaxed. "But I think it unwise to rely too heavily on the suggestions of any one mer. Let's consider your plan. Galena, what are your thoughts?"

Galena glanced at each face in the room as if trying to decide on the shrewdest course of action. "Your Highness, I think it's worth contemplating." She enunciated each word. "We would want to be careful to phrase it in such a way as to forestall any additional demands on their part. But I cannot imagine they really believe they'll get the full senate they're demanding. Unless they're just looking for an excuse to exact revenge, it seems to me that they might respond positively to such a compromise."

She pushed water through her gills. "Here's what I propose: Amnesty for all anti-monarchists who will take a pledge to unite with the city against an external threat. An offer of an elected senate that will remain subordinate to you in all that it does. And a promise that you will carefully consider all of the senate's recommendations."

I looked at Ti, but she had frozen with a neutral expression on her face. I tried to do the same.

Galena continued, "We should act sooner rather than later. Cleo is the most loyal citizen in the whole city—"

If only you knew.

"—but we cannot know how long she can bear up under torture. Who knows what lies they're telling her to try to convince her that the crown has turned on her and left her and her whole family for dead?"

My head snapped up, and I searched out Galena's eyes. She looked at me for just a moment, but I saw a flash of compassion and understanding in them.

She does know.

Elias seemed to comprehend her point. "Well . . . it seems a harmless enough compromise to me, all things considered. Let's send out the crier. We'll set the elections for one month hence."

Barnabas shot upward, "Your Highness—"

But Elias held up his hand for silence. "I don't want to hear another word on this subject from you. I am the king."

He's trying to imitate his father. A swell of pity rose within me. We'd all dreaded the day when Elias would ascend the throne. His wavering, uncertain personality coupled with his impulsivity had always been a toxic combination. And now that he was adding false bravado to the mix, I feared we were in for deadly currents. But perhaps, with sound counsel, we could hold off the catastrophe that loomed before us. This time.

And perhaps we could get Mother back. I reached out toward Benjamin. "Let's go home, urchin," I murmured in his ear.

Ti followed us out the door, and we began our subdued trip home.

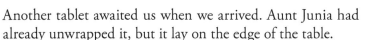

Another tablet awaited us when we arrived. Aunt Junia had already unwrapped it, but it lay on the edge of the table.

C is alive.

I clutched it to my chest and made eye contact with Orua, who was back on duty.

"What does it say?" asked Benjamin.

"It says that Mother is alive."

"From Maximus?"

My head snapped toward him. "Did you see Maximus? While you were being held?"

He nodded. "He snuck in to see me twice. We were making an escape plan when Faustus and Carlina decided to let me go."

"Carlina?"

With a shrug, Benjamin said, "She's up there in the ranks. Nicer than Faustus is."

I studied him. "Do you know where they're keeping Mother?"

He shook his head. "They moved her before they released me."

But maybe Maximus knows now.

Mother had been right. The anti-monarchists had given up Benjamin in exchange for something more valuable— Cleo and her information. I wondered what Mother had told them to convince them she was serious about doing anything in her power to save her son.

I wondered what she was telling them now, under threat of the anti-monarchists coming after her children again.

And I wondered how much Elias and his advisors had figured out about her actions.

I wished I could send a return tablet to Maximus, to plead for more information, but we hadn't set up a channel to allow for that. Besides, there was too much risk that the questions would fall into the wrong hands and betray Maximus.

I pushed water through my gills. I hated waiting.

"Benjamin!" Aunt Junia fairly flew up the corridor toward

him, as if her joints didn't pain her at all. Perhaps in that moment, seeing him home safe, they didn't.

She wrapped her arms around his neck and kissed the top of his head until he shrugged out of her embrace.

"I'm safe," he said. "Really. Everything's fine."

Except that Mother's still missing.

And the worst part is, even if she came home safe, I didn't know how she'd be treated by the monarchy.

"Where's Alexander?" I asked.

"He and Pippa went out to buy some food," said Aunt Junia. "I expect they'll be back soon."

As if on cue, someone began pounding on the door. "Junia!" a female voice screamed.

It was Pippa.

The desperate timbre of her cry sent my head spinning, and I bolted to the door and unlocked it.

Pippa tumbled in, her hair and clothes in disarray.

"What's happened?" I asked. I looked behind her, but Alexander was nowhere to be seen. Panic flared in my chest.

She looked at me with wide, wild eyes. "They attacked us. Alexander's hurt."

TEN

Alexander's hurt.

The words hovered between us for a strangled, horrifying moment. Visions of Alexander wounded and dying, of blood in the water, flickered in my head. A chill washed over me.

Then I snapped myself out of my reverie and stuffed down my emotions. "Where? What happened?"

Pippa's hands clenched together until they turned white. "He hit his head. It didn't look good. I got him to the house of healing."

I was already heading for the door.

"Wait." Pippa grabbed my arm. "Be careful. Take a guard."

Orua moved forward, her fist clasped to her heart. "I'll go."

"Who attacked you?" I asked Pippa, trembling.

Pippa shrugged, but her eyes were still wide. "They didn't . . . say. I didn't recognize any of them. I . . . "

I assumed anti-monarchists, but they weren't the only rabble in the city. But no matter who it was, an attack raised the question of *why*. With everything going on, why target Alexander and Pippa? They had bigger fish to catch.

Like trying to get the crown prince to establish a senate.

But I didn't have time to figure out why. Alexander was in the house of healing, and Orua would protect me on the way there.

I looked at the other soldier. "Guard them with your life."

He clasped his fist to his heart and bowed.

Orua and I flitted out the door and down the canal as quickly as we could. We weren't far from the house of healing, but my eyes darted this way and that as we intersected each canal.

"It doesn't make any sense," I murmured.

"What doesn't?" asked Orua.

"For the anti-monarchists to attack them."

Orua shrugged. "Revenge? They were pretty angry about Andronicus." After a moment, she added, more quietly, "I would be, too."

I winced. She voiced her discontent entirely too often to be safe. "Yeah . . . but Pippa and Alexander? That suggests someone angry with us. With our family specifically. Not with the crown prince. The crown prince barely knows that Pippa and Alexander exist."

"Well, who is angry with Cleo? Or with you?"

We turned a corner, and I tossed the question around in my mind. "Perhaps the anti-monarchists, but I can't imagine they'd come after us like this when they have Mother."

"Who else?"

"Well, you can't be as powerful as Mother has been in Thessalonike without making enemies. She's expelled people. Ended careers. It could be Darius Vanapolos's family. Or . . ."

Or Felix.

"Or who?"

Pieces came together in my head. Felix undoubtedly hated us. We'd torn apart his family and exposed his corrupt business dealings.

More than that, Pippa was the sister of the naiad who had unleashed the whole sequence of events after she'd become suspicious of Felix and snooped through his business records.

Tor had said she'd tried to extort the family, but I'd never believed that. But as she'd investigated, she'd discovered a bone-chilling truth: Felix was abducting naiads and selling them as slaves—an offense punishable by the severest of consequences.

And my romance with Alexander had been kindled in the aftermath, while Tor's trial was still ongoing.

Yes, Felix probably hated all of us. And he had the means to hire mercenaries who would be written off as bitter anti-monarchists.

It wasn't proof, but it rang true.

"Perhaps Felix," I whispered to Orua.

A troubled expression overtook her face. "That makes more sense." She hesitated. "Do you really think he killed Yvonna?"

"Yes."

"Why?"

"Why do I think it? Or why did he do it?"

She shrugged. "Both, I guess. That one never made any sense to me either."

I struggled to shift my focus to Orua's questions, but I kept picturing Alexander dying in the house of healing. I sped up, and Orua matched my pace.

Finally, I said, "You remember the trial? Tor's trial?"

"Of course. Doesn't everyone?"

"And the talk that Felix was involved in some shady business dealings?"

She nodded.

"Well, he was. And Yvonna found proof of it. She came to me with it and was murdered the next day."

Orua pushed water through her gills. "Well. That is damning, isn't it?"

"Seems to be."

I caught a glimpse of the house of healing in the distance and increased my pace again.

I'm coming, Alexander.

I couldn't stand the thought that he'd come back to Thessalonike for me only to be gravely injured or . . .

No, not worse. I'm not going to lose him.

He'd make it. He had to.

"I'm sorry about Alexander," murmured Orua, taking in the expression on my face.

Orua, of all mermaids, understood my turmoil. Maximus was risking his life to infiltrate the anti-monarchists. Surely she fully knew the agony I was feeling.

Normally, this canal would be crowded, but the uncertainty in the city still motivated most to stay inside and out of the canals. It wasn't completely empty—after this many days, mer had to run some errands—but I could count the mer in my line of vision on two hands.

As we drew closer and closer to the house of healing, the vise on my chest tightened. What would we find when we arrived?

Orua reached out and rested her hand on my back as we surged forward parallel to the seafloor.

I didn't respond—I hardly knew how—but I hoped she knew how grateful I was that she'd been on duty when we'd received the news. That she'd rallied to my aid even after my role in endangering Maximus.

There was no other member of the Guard I'd rather have had with me.

I pounded on the doorway to the house of healing, and a white-clad merman opened it. He looked us up and down as if to assess whether we were sick or injured, and then asked, "How can I help you?"

"My-my fiancé was hurt. You're treating him." Technically, I didn't know if Alexander and I were really engaged. We had been once . . . and we hadn't really readdressed that conversation yet. But it seemed wrong, dismissive somehow, to just call him my *friend*. Fiancé would do.

He tilted his head. "What's your fiancé's name?"

"Alexander. Alexander Adrianopolos."

He moved to the side and allowed us to come in to the entry room. "I'm sorry," he said. "We're just being a little more careful right now."

"I understand," I said softly.

"Wait here." He held up his hand. "I'll go check on Alexander's progress and see if he's able to have any visitors yet." He turned and floated down the coral corridor.

Yet. I clung onto that word with every inch of my being, hoping against hope that it really meant he was going to be okay.

I'd been in such a hurry to find him that I hadn't pressed Pippa for more information about the extent of his injuries, and I'd been imagining the worst.

But Pippa's pale face and trembling hands when she'd told me said more than words. I begged the tides that we weren't about to get devastating news, but I knew that we weren't about to get anything approximating *good* news.

When was the last time we'd gotten genuinely good news, after all?

Orua squeezed my hand until it hurt. The pain helped bring my focus back down to the present moment, away from the visions of death and destruction playing out in my head.

I squeezed back until I thought the bones in my hand might break.

The merman turned back into the corridor and swam toward us.

Bile rose in my throat.

"Your young man is still alive," he said in an even, steady voice when he swept into the room. "The physician's best guess is that he will remain that way, but he's not out of danger yet."

"What happened?" I clasped my left hand behind my neck.

"He was shoved backward into a stone building. His head struck the rock hard, and he lost consciousness. He's bled a great deal, and he hasn't woken up yet."

"Can I see him?" My voice squeaked.

He shook his head. "Not yet, I'm afraid. The physician is still working on him and can't be disturbed. But you're welcome to wait here."

I dug my fingernails into the skin of my neck. "How long?" I'd spent so depths long waiting to see if the people I loved most in the world were going to be okay. Benjamin. Mother. Now Alexander.

I was about to snap.

"Certainly by the end of the day," he said.

I didn't even know what time it was. So much had happened, and everything was blending together.

I scanned the room for a tide glass, and my eyes settled on one in the corner. Three-quarters of the way to low tide. And the sun wouldn't set until just before low tide today.

I gave him a curt nod and floated toward the window to stare out at the canal.

Behind me, Orua murmured, "Can you let us know if anything changes?"

"Of course," the merman said.

I sensed Orua swim up behind me.

"I'm sorry," I said.

"Sorry for what?"

"I sent Maximus into danger, and now I can't handle the idea that Alexander's hurt."

"Jade." Her voice took on a chiding tone that somehow reminded me of Mother. "Maximus's job puts him in danger every day. And he went to save a life—because it was the right thing to do. I was angry earlier, but I shouldn't have been. Maximus is a grown merman. He makes his own choices."

Even if he doesn't come back home? I didn't say it aloud

because it seemed simultaneously self-absorbed and unhelpful. Orua didn't need to contemplate that possibility, just like I didn't need to imagine the white-clad merman telling us Alexander wouldn't survive.

A knock sounded on the front door, and the merman came back down the corridor and answered it, admitting a mother and her young son, who had gotten a dozen urchin quills stuck in his hand. The merman guided them down the hall and into a presumably empty room.

Before low tide, four other mer had come into the house of healing, and three had left.

Despite the fear in the canals, the city continued on as it always did.

The crier swam down the canal outside, announcing the king's plan to establish a council of advisors elected democratically. I hoped word had already gotten to the anti-monarchists.

Then, just as the tide glass began to fill up again, signaling the move toward high tide, the merman laid a hand on my shoulder. "The physician has done all he can for now. Your fiancé is still unconscious, but we're hoping he'll wake up soon. You can go to him if you'd like."

Orua and I soared down the corridor ahead of the physician's assistant. As I reached the corridor of patient rooms, I paused and spun back around to ask what room Alexander was in.

The assistant gestured ahead of us and to the left, and we swept into a room with yellow coral walls. Alexander lay on the hammock bed on the far side.

His face was pale, and his eyes remained closed, but his gills pulsed in strong, steady movements.

"Alexander." I flew to his side and threaded my fingers through his.

He didn't respond, but he was alive.

Orua remained behind me, as if giving us space. I turned

my head toward her. "Thank you for coming. I . . . I don't know how I would have endured the wait without you."

"I can wait outside the door if you'd like," she said.

"No. That wasn't what I meant at all."

I beckoned her forward, and she sank down onto the floor next to me. "Stay here with me until your shift is over and someone else comes to take your place."

We held each other's gaze, and something poignant passed between us—a mutual understanding, perhaps, or respect. A knowledge that we could count on each other for support in the middle of the dangerous days ahead, as we and the people we loved found ourselves in deeper water than we'd ever bargained for.

Alexander's room didn't have windows, and I wasn't keeping track of time, but my guess was it was starting to get dark outside when he stirred.

I tightened my grip on his hands. "Alexander? Can you hear me?"

He fell still again, and disappointment gripped my frame. But then I felt a slight pressure on my hands.

"Alexander?"

This time he opened his eyes—not all the way—and murmured, "Jade?"

Emotion bubbled in my chest. "It's me."

He almost smiled.

He'd come back to me.

"What are you doing here?" he asked, his voice still soft and weak.

"Waiting for you to wake up, silly." My voice cracked.

"Benjamin?"

"He's back home."

Confusion flooded Alexander's face, like it took him an extra beat to piece my words together. "And your mother?"

"Still no word."

At least not that anyone's notified me of. But I couldn't focus on that right now. I thought back to the way I'd acted . . . well, just a few weeks earlier, really. How it had seemed like the whole weight of the world rested on my shoulders. And now I had to accept that I couldn't even save my own family, much less the city.

But I could wait at Alexander's bedside.

"She'll be okay." Alexander looked up at me.

I almost laughed. Even injured in a bed in the house of healing, his first instinct was still to comfort and reassure me. I didn't deserve him.

And he certainly deserved better than me and all the uncertainty that I brought along with me, but I was grateful he'd chosen me anyway.

I bent down and kissed his lips. He kissed me back, softly, but with a depth of passion behind it that sent quillpricks through me.

Orua cleared her throat, and Alexander and I broke away from each other.

I opened my mouth to apologize, embarrassed, but Orua just shook her head, her face straining as if suppressing a grin. "You guys are cute, you know that?" Then a shadow passed over her face. "But my shift's just about up, and I need to rest between shifts."

I reached toward her. "Go in peace. Thank you for everything."

"Peace be—"

Movement blurred in the doorway, and Orua's hand flew to her side.

I blinked. I couldn't process what I was seeing. There was something sticking out of her waist . . . *a spear.* Blood pooled out of the wound and turned the water red around her torso.

I whirled back toward the door where the spear had come from, but there was no one there. It had been a targeted attack.

"Help!" I shrieked. "Someone help us." I swam to Orua and helped guide her down to the floor, then put my hands over the wound, around the base of the spear. I didn't want to damage her further by pulling it out.

Blood flooded my gills, and I clamped them closed to keep from choking on it.

A mermaid and a merman appeared in the doorway, and I glanced up wildly toward them. But they were just two assistants to the physicians.

"She was attacked," I squeaked. "Get help."

The merman disappeared from the doorway, and the mermaid came toward us, an alarmed expression etched on her face.

"What happened?" She bent over the wound and inspected it. Her lips twisted.

"I . . . don't know. Someone came in and . . . speared her. I-I didn't get a good look at them." I was blubbering now, but I didn't care. They'd come for Orua. Right in front of me. In the house of healing. And we hadn't been able to do anything about it.

Orua's lips had gone pale.

"What's her name?" asked the assistant.

"Orua," I whispered.

"Orua." She snapped her fingers in front of Orua's eyes. "I'm Syra. Stay with us, okay? Stay awake for just a little longer. We're here. We've got you."

Orua's eyes were foggy, as though she weren't all there.

Two physicians burst into the room.

"Status?" one barked.

"She's bleeding out," said Syra. "Spear wound. We're staunching it as best we can."

One of the physicians crossed over to Orua while the other began unraveling a pile of bandages.

"Give us the room," the first physician said to me as she took my place at Orua's side.

Hesitantly, I pulled my hands back from Orua's wound and backed away. For the first time since Orua had been speared, I looked up at Alexander through the haze of red. He'd lost consciousness again.

I wanted to scream, but I couldn't distract the physicians from their work. Slowly, I swam toward the door and into the corridor.

Another assistant passed me carrying an armful of medical supplies, and I hoped it would be enough. The wound had looked deep. My hands felt heavy with blood, somehow, and I wanted to scrub it off. Maybe then I'd wake up from this nightmare.

Had she been attacked by the anti-monarchists? Had they found out Maximus's true aims in joining them?

Almost aimlessly, I swam down the corridor to the door into the canal. I reached for the handle and wrenched it open. Then I floated out and sank down onto the step just outside the door. Maybe I wasn't being *safe*, but nothing was *safe* anymore.

Our home had been poisoned in the middle of the night. Benjamin had been snatched from behind a locked door. Orua had been speared within the walls of the house of healing.

Safety was a farce. An illusion.

I supposed I was starting to get a taste of what the naiads had endured for years. I understood why the liberationists had begun attacking mer. Why they'd rioted.

Depths, *I* wanted to riot.

I rubbed my hands together trying cleanse them of the blood, but they were still red. With a deep, guttural sigh, I leaned forward, trying to still my racing heart.

I was so sick of all of it. But what could I do?

I slumped back against the step. Not much. But then the vaguest of ideas took hold in the back of my mind. Maybe I couldn't do anything to save Orua or to protect . . . well, anyone, really. But I could do one small thing to help rid the city of this murderous element that threatened us all.

I floated upward and turned right to swim down the canal. The sooner the inspectors were informed of what had happened to Orua, the sooner they could begin an investigation to bring the would-be assassin to justice. I hadn't seen who had done it, but surely someone had seen *something* out of the ordinary.

We'd find the mer who had tried to kill her. And we would sink them to the depths.

⌒

The inspectors' offices were dank and chilly, just as I remembered. As I crossed the threshold, waves of memories washed over me. My numb disbelief when Father died. The cold determination I'd felt while reporting Anna's murder.

Happy memories weren't formed in the inspectors' offices.

I took in the dull gray walls—austere, as always—the table on the left side of the room, and the corridor that stretched backward to rooms I hadn't seen either heartbreaking time I'd come here.

This time, Inspector Leo was floating behind the table, looking over a set of tablets scattered across it.

"Hi," I said hesitantly.

He looked up at me and rolled his eyes. "You again? Reporting another murder, are we?"

I winced. "I hope not."

That got his attention. He studied me carefully. "What is it?"

"A member of the Royal Mer Guard was speared in the house of healing. She's hurt but still alive, last I saw her."

He rested a hand on the table. "The physicians are attending to her?"

"Of course."

He shuffled the tablets on the table and brought a blank one to the top, then reached for a scrib tucked behind his ear.

"Did you witness this?"

"Yes." I pressed my fingertips together.

"Name of the victim?"

"Orua . . . " I trailed off as I realized I didn't know her surname.

"Did you see the aggressor?"

I shook my head.

"You said this happened *in* the house of healing?"

"Yes, thank the tides."

"Did you notice what kind of spear it was?"

I thought about it and closed my eyes, trying to visualize the scene. Finally, I said, "I think it was a fisher's spear. The handle seemed shorter and thinner than the spears the guards carry when they patrol the wall."

Inspector Leo continued to jot down notes on his tablet.

"But the spear should still be there," I said. "The physicians hadn't removed it from her side when I left to tell you."

"Any other details you can remember?"

"No."

He wrote another note and set the tablet down. "Thank you for bringing this matter to our attention, Lady Jade. We'll take it from here."

I felt dismissed, and it stung, somehow. He knew I'd told the truth about Anna. The evidence had been clear enough. But I brushed aside the perturbed feeling and floated to the door and back out into the canal. I scanned from one side to the other, trying to decide what to do and where to go. Back to the house of healing, I supposed, to wait with Alexander and hope for news of Orua.

I traveled slowly, feeling dejected. How had it happened so fast? Why had they come for her? Had it been one of Felix's goons targeting me? Or had someone wanted to kill Orua?

I bit my lip and swam a little faster. If the same person who had attacked Alexander and Pippa had gone after Orua, Felix no longer seemed like the most likely culprit.

Given Mother's recent activities and Orua's thinly veiled discontent, I couldn't suppress a terrible suspicion: that Crown Prince Elias was trying to eliminate his critics.

CHAPTER

ELEVEN

I left the house of healing late that night and set off at dawn the next morning—over the protests of the soldiers guarding our home—to return to Alexander's side. When I was halfway there, movement to the left caught my eye, and I glanced down the canal to make eye contact with Cassian. My heart pounded. What was *he* doing here, watching me?

Cassian was a mercenary who, last I talked to him, was trying to get ahold of the suspicious tablet from Felix's business records. He'd claimed that his employer was trying to bring Felix to justice, but I'd never been sure whether he was working for the king or Felix himself. Or someone else altogether.

I trained a cold gaze on him, and he shook his head and smirked but didn't move.

I turned right and swam toward the house of healing but came to a halt less than halfway down the canal. Cassian's appearance had startled me, but it couldn't be a coincidence. He'd wanted me to see him.

Who was he working for now?

No way to find out without asking him. And it wasn't as if I could hide from him forever. He'd proven himself more than able to infiltrate the places I'd thought safe.

And by now I knew that nowhere was safe. There was no place I could go that they couldn't find me.

The thought was both terrifying and freeing.

I slowly turned around swam back until I found Cassian, still hovering where I'd left him.

With slow, deliberate strokes, I moved toward him, keeping a fierce expression on my face. When I was still about a dozen tail-lengths from him, I halted. "Why are you here?"

He smirked, and it infuriated me. "Milady. What a surprise."

"Is it, though?"

"No."

"Do you need something from me, or do you just want me to know I'm being watched?"

He shrugged. "Me, personally? I'm indifferent. I don't care who runs the city. It's all the same to me."

"You know that isn't what I mean. You're here for a reason."

"Ah. My current employer."

"Are you being deliberately difficult?" I folded my hands, trying to avoid betraying any emotion. Besides irritation.

"No."

"The same employer you had last time we talked?"

He shook his head. "Ah, that one is currently . . . indisposed."

Well, that didn't help me narrow it down between Felix and the king. Both of them were arguably indisposed right now—the one under house arrest and the other in an arguably more permanent state of indisposition.

"So, who are you working for now?" I let a hint of accusation lace my voice. I had a couple of guesses, and none of them were good.

"Come, now, milady," he said with a sardonic smile. "Everyone's got to eat."

I chewed on the inside of my mouth. "So, again, why are you here?"

"Keeping an eye on you if you must know."

"Are you working for Faustus?" I asked.

His head jerked up. "What makes you ask that?"

So you are. "Do you know where Mother is?"

"That, I can give you an honest answer to—no, I do not."

"Do you know who does?"

He didn't reply.

A crazy thought took hold of me, and I swam closer to him. "Can you take me to her?"

He studied me as if trying to discern whether I was serious or not. "I might be able to take you to someone who *might* know where she is. But I doubt it's a lot you'd want to fall in with."

"For the last time." I thrashed my fin against the seafloor. "Why are you watching me? Or, rather, why did you want me to know I was being watched?"

"I'm not at liberty to say, naturally. I'm really not being coy just for the fun of it."

"Would your employer allow me to take you to him?"

Cassian tilted his head. "It's not forbidden."

"Please." I moved forward again until I was within reach. "I'm desperate for answers."

"If you come with me, you may regret your decision. Or not live long enough to do so."

My resolve wavered. If the anti-monarchists didn't kill me, Mother would.

But the beginnings of a plan were threading together in my head, and I didn't know whether I'd have another opportunity to execute it. Naturally, I wished I had more time—time to consult with Maximus and Orua and Alexander and Ti. Maybe even with Aunt Junia, although I didn't want to worry her more.

I stared at Cassian, hoping he could see my determination written on my face.

"You'll need to be blindfolded part of the way. Do you still want to come?"

Did I really want to face Faustus? I hoped I wasn't making the biggest mistake of my life. "Yes."

When Cassian ripped the blindfold off me, I found myself floating in front of a mermaid with teal hair and a beautiful face. She was young—just a few years older than me—and her deep-brown skin matched mine.

Her wrap was made of burlap but tied in an intricate pattern that left her shoulders bare.

Two broad-shouldered mermen carrying clubs flanked either side of her ornate chair. I didn't like the looks of them.

I met her wide, expressive eyes, and for a moment we said nothing.

Then, finally, I glanced back at Cassian and then up at the mermaid. "I'm looking for Cassian's employer."

The mermaid's laugh trilled through the water. "That would be me."

I blanched. This had not gone according to plan. He'd been taking me to Faustus . . . right? I pushed water through my gills.

"What did you want with Cassian's employer?" asked the mermaid.

"Are you working with the anti-monarchists?" I blurted.

She furrowed her brows. "Of course. Why were you so eager to see me if you knew so little about me?"

"I thought you were someone else."

"Well, that's flattering. Who did you hope to find?"

I hesitated. But I decided to be honest with her. Perhaps I'd get my audience with their leader after all. "Faustus."

Everyone—the mermaid, her guards, and Cassian—chuckled.

Heat flushed my face.

"You don't want to talk to Faustus, love," said the mermaid. "You're much safer with me."

"I'm not interested in being safe. I'm interested in finding my mother."

She narrowed her eyes. "You're Jade Cleopola." It wasn't a question.

"Yes."

"I'm Carlina Rosopola."

Carlina. Benjamin had mentioned someone by that name. Someone high up in the ranks of the anti-monarchists.

"Can you take me to Mother?"

A guarded expression stole over her face. "Your mother came to us willingly, Jade. She's in no danger."

"Faustus sent a note to the crown prince saying they'd torture her for information if Elias didn't institute a senate before the coronation."

She scoffed. "Faustus says a lot of things. He's an idiot. Go home, Jade, and stop meddling in our affairs. Your mother is perfectly safe."

"Why did you send Cassian to watch me?"

Carlina pressed the tips of her fingers together. "If you must know, so you'd lay low. But perhaps I underestimated you. You're a determined little urchin, aren't you?"

I said nothing.

"But you see the world so simply," she continued. "For you, the monarchy's all you've ever known and dreamed possible. I doubt you're really a bad sort of girl, but your imagination is limited."

"You know nothing about me," I retorted.

She studied me. "Well, that's an interesting response."

"You think that I blindly support the crown prince just because of who I am? He's a fool, and the king was a tyrant. I might support your movement if it weren't such a cesspool of violence," I spat.

Carlina leaned back in her hammock and studied her fingernails. "Perhaps you and I are not so different."

"I am *nothing* like you."

She laughed again. "You see, *Jade*, I'm not the webbed-foot dragon you think I am. Faustus is crazed, and so was Andronicus. Elements of our movement do terrible things. But I'm the voice of reason. I do my best to rein them in, and right now I'm trying to prevent them from the course of self-destruction they're on. Does that sound nothing like you?"

"The anti-monarchists don't care about the collateral damage they leave in their wake. You'll do anything as long as it furthers your aims, no matter how many lives you leave broken behind you." I raised my chin in a small act of defiance.

Her gaze softened. "I can see how the actions of Andronicus and Faustus would lead you to believe that, but one or two mer do not speak for us all."

"The leaders do not speak for the group?" I scoffed. You killed my father, and you kidnapped my brother. And killed George." I crossed my arms over my chest. "To say my mother came here willingly is a gross distortion of the truth. She would have never come here if she hadn't been desperate to save Benjamin."

A shadow crossed her face. "I'm very sorry for all the destruction that's been wreaked by some of our . . . most enthusiastic elements. Rest assured that I've dealt with the merman who killed your butler."

Confusion swirled inside me. "Dealt with him? How?"

She didn't respond, but the stern expression on her face told me all I needed to know.

"Does that make you any better than the king?"

"I take those kinds of offenses seriously. If we didn't restrain our own, then no, we wouldn't be any better than the king."

"You still kept Benjamin captive."

She gave a wry chuckle. "Faustus thought that was a good idea. I saw that no harm came to the boy and that he was swiftly released."

"Are you trying to tell me that you're just a well-intentioned revolutionary innocent of any wrongdoing?"

Carlina chuckled. "I'm quite well-intentioned, Jade. I'm also far from innocent."

The distinction seemed odd to me, but I let it go. Underneath Carlina's casual demeanor, I sensed an earnestness that confused me. And I was beginning to suspect that she'd wanted to talk to me. That she and Cassian had manipulated me into demanding an audience with her.

But no matter what Carlina said or did or intended, I wasn't going to leave without Mother—or at least without speaking to her. I slowed my pulsing gills and studied the room.

Carlina sat in a throne-like chair in the center of the otherwise plain room. The walls were made of sandstone, and something about the plain functionality of it reminded me of the time I'd spent in the old naiad quarter, before the naiads had moved on for the friendlier waters of Marbella.

I hoped the Neptunians were treating them as allies.

Then a new rage overcame me. Had the anti-monarchists driven the naiads out of Thessalonike just so they could take over the naiad quarter for their own uses?

Repulsive.

But I stilled the words that swelled up in my throat. Any number of buildings in the city had been built with plain stone. I had no reason to assume that we were in the naiad quarter.

But Cassian had brought me here through tunnels, and the naiad quarter had networks of those.

"Did you hear the crier today?"

Carlina arched an elegant eyebrow. "Yes. What of it?"

"The crown prince is willing to compromise."

"Faustus isn't," she said. "The crown prince has offered a pittance. There will be no peace in the city until there is true democracy."

Panic ripped through me. I had to establish some sort of rapport with her. Some sort of connection that might push her toward keeping Mother safe if Faustus decided to . . .

"Why don't I know you?" I asked.

She cocked her head. "Why would you?"

"You're, what, three or four years older than me? I don't remember you from school."

"Are you pretending to be naive or merely flaunting your ignorance?"

The words hit me like the tendrils of a stinging jellyfish. I held her gaze. "I don't know what you mean."

"Do you really think that every family in the city sends their children to school for more than a year or two? By the time my mother gave birth to her seventh child, they needed me at home to take care of the little ones," she spat. "Not that that's any of your business."

So much for establishing rapport. "Then why did you tell me?"

Her eyes narrowed. "You're as much of an enigma to me as I am to you."

We studied each other, and I broke the silence. "Is it for your siblings, then, that you joined the anti-monarchists? I can understand that."

"It's long past time we made a better world for all."

"And what about the naiads? Did your political movement make the world better for them?"

She shrugged. "The merman with whom you ought to take up that grievance is dead."

I wasn't sure if she meant Andronicus or King Stephanos. Perhaps both.

"You must understand, Jade, I didn't allow Cassian to bring you here so I could defend my every action—much less the actions of everyone associated with my group. I gave you this meeting so I could warn you to stay out of things that you can neither understand nor change."

But she hadn't just given me this meeting. She'd wanted it. I could see it in her eyes. Was she trying to gauge me?

"And why can't I understand it?"

"For the same reason your mother can't. You and I were born in different worlds. Perhaps we both have good intentions, perhaps in many ways we are similar, but we are at odds with each other because our beliefs are so diametrically opposed that there is no middle ground."

My exasperation grew too strong, and I thwacked my fin against the floor. "Why does everyone keep assuming I blindly support the monarchy even after I've said that I don't? I can be opposed to your violence—the violence that has torn apart my family—and still believe that one mer should not exercise total control over a city."

Something glimmered in her eyes, and I suspected she'd gotten what she was looking for.

"And what do you think you're playing at"—I crossed my arms—"seizing this opening right now, with the threat of invasion looming before us? Do you think that the Neptunians will be better overlords than Crown Prince Elias?"

"Well, they can hardly be worse," she muttered.

I shot her a sharp look. "And you criticize me for my naivete."

I knew I was treading dangerous waters, but I couldn't stop myself. I was talking to a leader of the anti-monarchists. Perhaps this was my one chance to talk reason into someone who might listen. The tides knew Elias wouldn't.

"Listen," I said, "if I'm being honest with you, I've harbored those thoughts, too. But do you think anyone who styles themselves after the ancient Neptunians has aims of benevolent rule?"

She laughed. "I don't care for fairy tales."

"Whether or not the Neptunians of old existed is beside the point. These mer have declared that they want to be like them. Do we want to risk the horrors of foreign rule on the off-chance that they might be sympathetic to your desire for a democracy? How many empires want democracy?"

"You'd be surprised."

"If the city is torn apart by infighting when the Neptunians arrive, we won't stand a chance."

She pushed herself upward and hovered over the ornate chair. "Then I suggest the crown prince negotiate a peace deal with us before the Neptunians take his throne by force."

TWELVE

"You'd risk all our lives for your political gambit?"

The guards on either side of Carlina glanced up at her, but she shook her head. "The Neptunians won't slaughter us. They have no reason to. They're interested in power, in tribute. They'll have no subjects if we're all dead. You, *milady*, are concerned about losing your comforts and way of life. We do not share your concerns."

"What if the Neptunians preserve the monarchy, subservient to themselves, and wipe out the revolutionaries?"

She tilted her head, still staring into my eyes. "And why would they do that?"

"Because the anti-monarchists have already proven willing to rebel against authority."

Uncertainty flickered in her eyes. I'd made my point.

"The monarchy may not have a secure net from which to bargain, but don't be fooled into thinking that you do. We *all* have a lot to lose."

Carlina shot me a dazzling smile and said in a languid voice, "Thank you for the warning, which I will certainly take under advisement. Now, go back to your fancy house and your old money with my personal assurance of your mother's safety."

"That's not good enough!" I shouted.

Her eyebrows flicked upward. "You do not come into my court and dictate to me. Here, in this room, I am as good as queen."

"Then how are you better than the monarchy?"

"Don't presume to lecture me." She sat up straighter.

"Is there any sort of compromise the anti-monarchists might agree to? Might you sit down and negotiate with the crown prince?"

Her eyes narrowed to slits. "No. Now, get out."

"I want to see my mother."

"Leave."

She nodded at Cassian, who still floated at the back of the room, and he moved forward with the blindfold in hand. For all my thoughts of bravery, I didn't protest as he looped it over my eyes, lightly placed his hand on my upper arm, and guided me into the darkness of what I presumed was a tunnel. When we'd been traveling for a few minutes, I murmured, "Do you want to be responsible for the death and destruction that awaits all of us if we cannot present a unified front against the Neptunians?"

"Milady, I do what I'm paid to do. Figuring out what course of action leads to death and destruction is not my concern."

"The naiads said you were an assassin. Is that true?"

He didn't hesitate. "I've killed before."

"How many?"

This time he paused for a fraction of a second before answering. "Once."

"And were you at peace with yourself afterward?"

"What is peace?"

We turned a corner and fell into uncomfortable silence.

At long last, we emerged into fresh canal water, and light filtered through my blindfold. "Just a little further," he said.

After we rounded another bend, he spun me around five or six times and removed the blindfold from my eyes. The canal around us was deserted, and I had no idea where we were. Sandstone buildings lined the street, and all appeared deserted. I couldn't see coral gardens in any direction, and seagrass lined the edges of the canal. A few small fish darted in and out of the seagrass.

"I trust you can find your way home from here," he said.

I opened my mouth, looked around again, and then closed it. Yes. I'd find my way home. "Go in peace," I said.

He didn't respond as he turned and swam away.

I sank down to the seafloor, my gills pulsing wildly. *Alexander. Orua.*

"Wait!"

He turned around and looked at me with an expression of supreme impatience.

"Orua and Alexander. Were you paid to hurt them?"

His expression didn't change. "I don't know who Orua is, and I don't care about the mermen you keep around. Peace, milady."

I spun away from him. I needed to get back to Orua and Alexander first, to find out if they were alright. If they were going to survive the day.

I swam until I reached an intersecting canal, and then I pulled myself up. I was in the old naiad quarter after all. I'd just reached Camford Canal, where I'd come with Pippa back before the massacre. Everything looked so different now that the naiads were gone and the canals were empty and desolate. Gathering my bearings, I turned to the right and swam toward where I thought the rest of the city lay. Though I briefly considered rising above the buildings to see the city from a higher vantage point, I shook the thought away. Better to risk wandering aimlessly for a few canals than to draw undue attention to myself.

The house of healing. I have to get to the house of healing.

Deep in my core, I thought Alexander would be alright. The physicians had said so. But Orua? It had been a lot of blood. I reached the end of Camford Canal, relieved to find myself staring at the boundary of the part of the city I knew so well. I could reach the house of healing from here. I surged forward, trying to move swiftly and silently now that I knew where I was. Several canals in, I turned onto Dolphin Canal. A few mer dotted the seascape here and there, but ordinarily this section of the city would be brimming with life and activity. The contrast was startling, a grave reminder that these weren't just dark tides for a few—the whole city was living in fear.

I hoped against hope that we'd look back on these days as a dark, fleeting memory, and not as the time when everything changed. But Carlina's words rang in my head.

You, milady, are concerned about losing your comforts and way of life. We do not share your concerns.

I knew there was decay at the center of the city's power structures. But I couldn't comprehend how deep that decay must go if so many mer were willing to risk the destruction of the city, of their loved ones, of their own lives to change things. Carlina believed in something. I . . . wished I could say the same.

What about democracy? I shook my head to try to banish the treacherous voice. I didn't believe in monarchy. Not anymore. But I couldn't bring myself to think that the will of the angry mob might be any saner than the will of an autocrat. Not after the violence and hatred I'd seen.

Another turn brought me in eyesight of the house of healing. Four members of the Royal Mer Guard were stationed outside the door. I hesitated, swimming more slowly toward them. I only vaguely recognized the soldiers.

One of them, a burly merman to whom I took an instant dislike, eyed me up and down as I approached the house of healing. "Are you hurt? What's your business here?" he barked.

"My fiancé is inside. He's injured." I thought it best not to mention Orua.

"What's your fiancé's name?"

"Alexander Adrianopolos. Why are you here? I've never seen a patrol stationed here before."

"I'll ask the questions." He rose up a half-tail length from the seafloor and hovered over me menacingly.

I glanced from one guard to the next, expecting someone to intervene, but they remained silent.

"I'd like to see my fiancé," I finally said.

The burly merman nodded at a hook-nosed mermaid, and she whirled around and went into the house of healing. We waited in awkward silence for a span of time that seemed to stretch out into oblivion, and then she reappeared in the doorway. "You may enter."

I glided past them, my head held high. When I entered the house of healing, I blinked against the dim light. A white-haired mermaid I didn't recognize waited at the front table. There had been a changing of shifts.

"You're here to see the young merman with the head injury?" she asked, gentleness in her gaze.

"Yes."

She rose up from her hammock chair. "He's stable. I'll take you to him."

"And Orua? The guard who was attacked? She's a friend."

She looked back at me, and compassion swelled in her voice. "Time will tell. I'm afraid she can't have visitors yet."

The blood drained from my face. "Is she dying?"

"It's too early to say what the outcome will be. Come. I'll take you to your young man."

"And the Royal Mer Guard at the door? Are they to protect Orua?"

She continued to glide down the corridor without turning to look at me. "They're to protect all of the sick and injured," she said, her voice steady and even. "Never before in our history have we suffered such an attack within our walls. As tensions continue to run high, we thought it best to take precautions."

We arrived at a different room from the one Alexander had been in before, and she gestured at the doorway.

I hesitated. "This is the one?"

"Yes. He's been in and out of consciousness all morning. A physician should be in soon to check on him, and he will be able to answer any questions you have."

Without another word, I turned and swam through the doorway. Alexander lay asleep on a hammock bed against the far wall. His gills pulsed in rhythmic, even movements, and I flew to his side and threaded my fingers through his. Touching him brought me comfort.

A little shudder wracked my body, and I laid my head against his chest. "The city can't take much more," I said. "We're caught in a torrent of our own making, and half the skubs in Thessalonike can't even see it."

He stirred, just slightly, but enough to send a thrill of hope through my body. "Please wake up," I whispered.

But he fell still again, only the gentle movement of his gills betraying signs of life.

"If one more thing goes wrong . . . " George's face flashed through my mind, and I longed for the presence of my second father. But he was gone. Carlina's people had killed him.

Don't give in to hate.

"I just wish I weren't so confused," I continued. I glanced at the tide glass on the wall. It was midday. The visit to Carlina had taken longer than I'd realized. If Alexander wasn't awake yet, he'd likely stay another night in the house of healing. I reached out and traced my fingers along his cheek, torn between staying at his side and returning home to Benjamin. Surely he was worried. I'd arrived home last night after he was asleep and left before anyone in the house was stirring. Likely, he was still processing the trauma of his abduction and captivity.

The Guard is outside. Alexander is safe here.

A rap sounded on the doorframe, and a physician entered

the room wearing the white wrap of the house of healing. She approached Alexander's bedside and leaned over to inspect the scabbed-over wound on his head. "Have you seen any change?" she asked.

"He moved a little."

"Good." She nodded. "He's been in and out of consciousness."

"The assistant told me."

I gripped his hand. Maybe he'd wake again soon, and I could tell him that I needed to go to Benjamin. "He's going to be okay?"

"He may have some memory loss from the blow to the head. And it's too soon to tell about the length of the recovery or whether there will be any lingering effects. But he'll live."

We could deal with the details as they came up. It was enough to know that he would live.

We conversed in low tones for a few more moments, and then she left to go check on her next patient.

I squeezed Alexander's hand again. "Please, wake up."

Another glance at the tide glass. Benjamin would be worried.

Alexander stirred again, and this time he opened his eyes. "You're back," he said with a wan smile.

My lip quivered. "I'm so happy you're awake."

"What happened to Orua?" he murmured. "I remember the blood . . ."

I chewed the inside of my cheek. "She was speared. She's being attended by the physicians. We have high hopes she'll make a full recovery." I wouldn't let go of that hope until I was presented with news to the contrary.

His mouth worked as though he couldn't quite form the words he wanted to say. Finally, he managed, "Who would have . . . wanted to hurt . . . Orua?"

It was the question I'd been trying to put out of my

head. I ran through my ideas again: Had the monarchy been informed of her less-than-loyal thoughts? Had the anti-monarchists targeted her for some reason? Had the spear instead been intended for me or Alexander?

I kept coming back to the crown prince.

What would Maximus do when he found out his beloved was grievously injured?

"I wish I knew." I stared at the light-blue coral wall. "Maybe it has something to do with the upheaval in the city. Maybe she has personal enemies."

"Benjamin is back?" he asked.

"Yes," I said. "You . . . are you having a hard time remembering?"

He wrinkled his forehead as he squinted at the ceiling. "It comes and goes, I think. You should be with him."

I dug my fingernails into my palms. "You need me."

He shook his head. "Benjamin needs you. He's so young. Cleo going to them . . . he needs you today."

The vise that had tightened around my heart loosened. I bent over and kissed his cheek. "I love you. I'll be back tomorrow as early as I can."

"I love you." He pulled my hand up to his lips and kissed my fingers.

With a final hurried goodbye, I left Alexander behind, swam down the corridor, and left by the front door, past the guards. For now, I was grateful they were there. With a little shiver, I swam down the canal, imploring the tides to keep me safe on my way back to Aunt Junia's.

THIRTEEN

A guard answered when I knocked on Aunt Junia's door. "Lady Jade," he said, moving aside to usher me in. He handed me another tablet, and I read it wordlessly, recognizing Maximus's scrawl.

Still haven't seen C.

I set the tablet down on the table with a little hiccup of disappointment. No one except the guards was in the front room, so I moved toward the corridor, my heart lurching painfully in my chest when I passed the spot where George had died.

I glanced in Aunt Junia's chamber. She lay asleep in her hammock. Grateful, I moved further down the corridor, to the room Benjamin had been staying in. I knocked on the doorframe and poked my head through the privacy screen. "Can I come in?"

He glanced up from where he sat in his hammock, his fin curled up underneath him and his arms hugging his body. A'a was curled up next to him. "Is Alexander okay?" he asked.

I eased into the room and swam up next to him. "Yes, he's going to be fine. A little confused from a blow to the head, but it's not as bad as we feared at first."

"Good," he said. "It feels like we're losing everyone." His voice cracked. "What if they kill Mother?"

"I talked to Carlina today. She swears that Mother is safe."

"You don't really believe that, do you?"

I thought about it. "I think Carlina believes it, and it's something we can hold onto for right now."

His lip quivered. "But what if she never comes home?"

"Hush." I pulled him into a tight hug. "You know it's not your fault that they have her, right?"

"It *is* my fault," he cried. "She gave herself up for me."

"Oh, urchin. They took you. It's their fault. Anything that happens is their fault. Not yours. Never yours."

"I want to believe that, but I can't."

I pulled away just far enough to look him in the eyes. "Would I lie to you?"

"Yeah."

I rolled my eyes. "But I'm not lying about this. Would you think it was my fault if the anti-monarchists had taken me, and Mother had offered herself up in my place?"

He considered the question, chewing on his bottom lip. "No."

"Then show yourself that same kindness, urchin. Nothing you did caused any of this."

"I miss George." He sounded like he was about to cry.

"I do, too, urchin. I do, too."

We sat in silence for a long time. At long last, he said, "Can we just talk about something? Anything good. Anything that doesn't have to do with what's happened."

I readjusted my arm around his shoulders, and A'a woke up. With a lazy curl of his tail, he climbed up the hammock to me and lumbered into my lap.

"Can you believe I adopted a dragon?" I asked.

He snorted. "Absolutely. You picked the right one. He's good company."

"I don't know what we'll do when he's bigger. He's never going to be able to swim straight with that lame fin, and he's hard enough to keep under wraps when he's small."

He shrugged. "You're, what? Sixty-seventh in line for the

throne? Maybe you'll be queen someday and make all the rules."

"One hundred and sixty-seventh last I heard. If I were merely sixty-seventh, I might be tempted to make a play for the crown."

"Well, I'm one hundred and sixty-eighth, then. You'd have to watch your back if you were queen. *I* might want to make a play for the crown." He winked at me.

"Nah." I reached out to ruffle his uncharacteristically un-coiffed hair. "A crown would mess up your hair too much."

He scowled. "At least I don't think about my wraps all the time. You'd be an insufferable queen."

"Well, lucky for you, I have no such designs. Besides, it'd be much easier to become queen by marrying Theo and waiting out Elias than by waiting for one hundred and sixty-seven people to die, and Theo and I wouldn't make a good match."

He paused and reached out to pet A'a on the chin. "Are you going to marry Alexander?"

Yes. Maybe? I hope so. "If he'll have me, I think so."

"Good. I'd like to have Alexander for a brother. Even if Mother doesn't like it."

"I think there are a lot of things Mother will care a whole lot less about once all this is over. And the social status of my husband is probably one of them. She only ever cared about it because she was afraid it would make my life harder if I married him." I elbowed Benjamin in the ribs. "So who knows, you may get to marry Isa Petrapola after all."

His face turned red, and he looked down at the floor. "I don't even like her anymore."

"Oh, who's the new lucky lady?"

"No one," he muttered.

"Uh-huh. I'll figure it out. I always do."

We fell asleep leaning against each other's shoulders like

we had when we were little kids, and for a brief span of time I could pretend that the world was right again.

⌒

The next morning, I made breakfast for Benjamin, Aunt Junia, Pippa, and Senator Ti.

"Are you going to the house of healing?" Pippa asked, nibbling on the edge of a crab-meat pod.

I nodded.

Benjamin reached out and gripped my forearm. "Do you have to?" he asked, his voice pleading.

I stared into his fathoms-blue eyes, "I'm sorry, urchin. I have to see Alexander and find out how Orua is. I'll come back to you. I promise."

Ti glanced from Benjamin to me. "Still, you ought not go alone. You know as well as any of us that it's unsafe."

"I'll go," said Pippa.

"Are you sure?" I set down my pod and studied her. "I don't want to put you at risk."

"I'm sure. We're all in this together. We all have to take risks."

Something in the intensity of her gaze stilled my protest. We ate in near silence, and when I set down half my pod uneaten—I didn't think I could stomach another bite in my anxious state—Pippa nodded at me and pushed up from the table. I rose, hovering a half-head above Benjamin, and then reached out to ruffle his hair. "We'll get through."

I wished I could offer him more certain comfort.

Without another word, Pippa and I departed for the house of healing.

A few more mer were out in the canals today. I supposed fear couldn't choke the city indefinitely.

"After we visit Alexander and Orua," I said, "perhaps we should slip out onto the reef to see Kiki."

A smile rose to the corners of her lips. "I'm sure she'd love that."

I swam a little faster. "I know we shouldn't leave the city, but I was gone to Marbella for so long and only briefly saw Kiki when I arrived home." Had that really only been four days ago? Or maybe not. It was all blending together. "Besides, I get some of my best ideas out on the reef with Kiki. Maybe we'll come back to the city afterward with a brilliant way to rescue Mother."

"Maybe."

I couldn't quite read the expression on her face. Trepidation, perhaps? Or resignation.

The brilliant sunlight filtering through the water buoyed my spirits as we sailed down the canal toward the house of healing.

We would figure this out. We would be okay. Things couldn't ever truly return to normal, but we'd find a new normal. We all would.

But first, we had to get Mother back. Pippa ground to a halt on the sandy seafloor, and a flicker of movement behind me caught my attention. I pulled up short and turned to find Cassian watching me. I rolled my eyes and waved at him, and with a wry smile, he gave a half wave in my direction.

"Let's go," Pippa whispered. "We don't know why he's here, and I'd rather not find out."

She was right, but something in his expression arrested me. *If only Cassian could be persuaded to help.* I'd puzzle out that idea on the reef. *What are the anti-monarchists paying him?*

With a tug on my arm, she drew me onward, and I turned back around, glancing at Cassian as we rounded a bend out of sight. I tried to put the encounter out of my head as we swept past the guards unchallenged into the house of healing. But why *was* he back so soon?

Pippa opted to stay in the front room. "Take all the time you need," she said. "If I wasn't waiting here, I'd just be waiting at your home. It's all any of us can really do."

"Thank you." I reached out and squeezed her hand for the briefest of moments before I was ushered back to Alexander's room by a familiar-looking merman.

"How is Orua, the guard who was attacked here yesterday?"

His face turned almost gray. "She still can't have visitors. We cannot yet speak confidently of the outcome."

The thin tendril of anxiety that had threaded its way through my chest grew into a pulsing sea urchin that threatened to swallow my heart. How I wished I had a way to send word to Maximus.

This time, Alexander was already awake, and color had returned to his face.

"How do you feel?" I asked, lunging to his side. I needed good news.

"Like a shark attack," he said.

"That bad?" I looked over his wound. "It seems like it's already starting to heal."

"It itches like it's healing. I'm still a little confused sometimes, and I have a pounding headache."

"Did you sleep last night?"

"Soundly. You?"

"Benjamin and I were up late talking, but yes. Eventually." In truth, anxiety had jolted me awake in the dark watches of the night, and I'd spent a lot of time at the window, looking out at the canal, wondering where Mother was and whether she was awake. Or at least alive.

"You look as though you haven't slept."

"You're as perceptive as George." Loss sliced through my heart yet again. I wondered when I'd be able to think of George without the searing pain of grief. If the heartache of Father's death was any indication, it'd be months. Or years.

Alexander's lips turned up in a sad, tender smile. "That's one of the highest compliments you could pay me."

We talked until almost midday, and then Alexander's eyes grew heavy. "I think I need to sleep more," he said. "Come see me again this evening?"

"Of course."

I waited until he fell asleep and then met Pippa in the front room.

"How is he?" she asked.

"In reasonably good spirits," I said. "Still no news of Orua?" I glanced from Pippa to the assistant sitting at the nearby table.

"Nothing to report yet," said the assistant. "But don't lose hope."

I nodded, chewing my lower lip, and turned away. "Let's go see Kiki," I whispered to Pippa.

I shouldn't have been surprised when I felt a heavy hand clamp down on my shoulder before we even reached the first corner. Somehow, I knew who it was without turning around.

"Cassian. What do you want this time?"

His smooth voice lacked the cynicism it had exuded the day before. "I suspect that you will find something of interest to you if you go to the king's court now."

"And why are you telling us this?" Pippa snapped.

"Because I also suspect that I am more likely to get paid what is owed me if the lady goes to the king's court now."

I turned around and stared at him. "Would you care to elaborate on that?"

"No."

"Riveting speech." Pippa folded her arms across her chest.

"I try."

I searched his face to try to find any hint of guile or genuineness, but he remained a mystery to me. "What will I find at court?"

"My employer."

"Carlina?"

"As you say."

Part of me wanted to give his navy-blue hair a sharp tug, as if I were still a schoolchild frustrated with vague answers. But more of me was intrigued with the information he'd given me. Carlina was at court? Why? "Is she in trouble?"

"I think it would be advantageous to both of us if you were to go there at once."

Which meant Cassian thought it would advantage *him* if I were to go there. But I couldn't deny the intrigue and concern that pulsed through my veins at the thought of Carlina facing down Elias. Elias wasn't likely to get the better of a verbal exchange. Not with someone as sharp-witted as Carlina. But Elias had the Royal Mer Guard at his disposal. And if Carlina had been telling the truth, that she was a moderating influence among the anti-monarchists, her death or banishment could put Mother in jeopardy.

It would also put Cassian's payment in jeopardy.

"Why did you come to me?" I asked.

"Because you act without thinking, and I needed someone to act."

"Thanks for the vote of confidence."

"Anytime."

"I'll do it if you'll help me get Mother out."

He tilted his head, as if he hadn't considered this possibility, but the expression on his face looked almost bored. He'd expected this.

"If you free Carlina, and your mother is still in their custody tomorrow, I will do what I can to help free her. It will also cost you a thousand drachmas."

"Yes," I said. "I'll pay it."

"I will leave you now." In a flash, he'd turned around and darted around a corner and out of sight.

"What do you think?" Pippa asked, her face hard. "Will he follow through?"

I pressed my fingertips together and gazed in the direction of the city gate. "Soon, Kiki," I murmured. "Soon."

With a rueful moan, I turned to Pippa. "Come with me?"

"Of course," she said, sounding tired.

My heart pounded as we turned toward the spires of the palace. Instead of floating with my dolphin, we'd be swimming with sharks.

CHAPTER

FOURTEEN

"For the last time," Elias thundered as Pippa and I entered court. "Why shouldn't I have you killed where you float?"

A mermaid's voice answered in softer tones that I couldn't quite make out.

Elias hovered in front of Carlina, several tail-lengths away from his chair at the base of the throne. His guards flanked him more closely than usual, and another pair boxed her in from behind.

"I do *not* negotiate with revolutionaries!" screeched Elias as he backhanded her across the face. She drifted backward, but she couldn't go far without colliding with the guards.

I blanched and searched for Barnabas—*was this his influence?*—but I couldn't find him.

I started forward again, Pippa at my side, wracking my brain for a plan. Cassian was right. I did act without thinking. And I was distinctly concerned it was about to get me in a great deal of trouble. "Your Majesty," I cried, swimming toward the front of the room. "Someone in the canal told me you had news of Mother. I came as fast as I could." I stopped alongside Carlina, who cast me a perplexed look out of the corner of her bruised eye. He'd hit her more than once.

Pippa halted a half-tail length or so behind me.

"What are you talking about?" Elias scoffed.

I mustered a tragic expression. "You mean you don't?"

He gestured with his chin. "This revolutionary might."

I whirled around to face her. "You're one of the anti-monarchists? Do you know where Cleo is?"

If Carlina was the moderating influence she said she was, I had to make sure she got out alive.

"It is information I'd be willing to trade," she said slowly. "For something equally valuable."

"Are you torturing her?" I asked, assuming what I hoped looked like a threatening posture.

She squared her shoulders. "I assure you she's being treated better than I am. But I'm not at liberty to discuss her further unless the crown princeling here agrees to negotiate a compromise."

Elias sputtered. I suspected Carlina had been talking circles around him for a while. I had to get her out before he killed her.

"Your Majesty," I said, as if the idea had just struck me. "Might the naiad and I have a private word with the revolutionary?"

He stared at me. "Why?"

"Your Majesty." Though I felt deadly calm, I let my voice crack as if I might be about to burst into sobs. "I'm desperate. They've had my mother for two days now. I can't sleep at night imagining what they might be doing to her. Please, just let me talk to the mermaid."

He waved his hand. "You may use one of the chambers there." He motioned with his hand to the doors to his left. "But she is not to leave court under any circumstances."

Carlina swam alongside Pippa and me willingly but with wide eyes. Well, one eye wide anyway. The other was starting to swell shut. I reached the ornately carved door, opened it, and motioned them both through it. After they swam into the small council chamber, I followed them in and closed the door behind us.

The room was sparsely furnished, with a handful of

ornately carved hammock chairs in a semicircle and a table at the far end. But the ceiling vaulted high above us. A small window near the top let in enough light to see by, but three thin lines of bioluminaries graced the wall halfway between the floor and ceiling.

"What the depths are you doing?" I hissed to Carlina. "He'll kill you. And then where will your movement be?"

She stared at me. "I didn't come here willingly, Jade. They found me. He'll probably sink me off the drop-off by sundown."

I bit down hard on my lip. *What might the anti-monarchists do in retaliation?* "Then what were you doing blustering about a negotiation?"

Pippa looked back and forth between us, but there was no time to explain how Carlina and I knew each other.

Carlina shrugged. "I figured I might as well try to negotiate before they killed me. Seemed better than just giving up and dying. What did you mean by hauling me in here?"

"To figure out what to do!"

"Didn't *you* want me to come here to negotiate? Wasn't that your suggestion?"

I searched my memory. I had said something like that, but . . . "I didn't mean just floating into court all by yourself."

"What's your angle on this? Why do you care so much?"

She and I stared at each other, unblinking. I couldn't tell her that Cassian had agreed to help me free Mother in exchange for Carlina. Finally, I glanced back at the door. "Because a lot of what you said yesterday rang true. And I think you may be my best chance at getting Mother back. And the city's best chance of making peace before the Neptunians come."

"I might have been lying to you."

"You weren't. Do they know where you live?"

"Yes. They came for me at home."

"I can hide you," I said.

Pippa shot me a glare.

Carlina stared past me. "That doesn't solve the immediate problem of getting out of here. Besides," she added in a sardonic tone, "what use can I be in your goal of uniting the city if I'm in hiding?"

"More use than you can be dead." Not to mention that I was afraid of what would happen to Mother if Carlina was killed.

What was I about to sacrifice? My life, possibly. Crown Prince Elias would very likely see the aiding and abetting of a high-ranking anti-monarchist as treason.

And now that Marbella was overrun, I didn't have anywhere to flee if it became too dangerous for me to stay.

I steeled myself. What was I hoping to accomplish?

Save Carlina's life. Rescue Mother. Survive this moment. Worry about the rest later.

I could imagine the lecture Pippa was giving me in her head. Something about my impulsivity and the way I bumbled everything up while trying to save the world.

Not the world. Carlina's right. She may not be able to negotiate a peace in hiding. But maybe I can save Mother. The world will have to take care of itself.

FIFTEEN

My mind flitted from plan to plan, discarding each as quickly as I mustered it. Elias didn't value my life enough for Carlina to use me as a hostage. I didn't think I could cause a big enough distraction to capture the attention of all the guards in the room long enough to allow her to escape. Perhaps we could outswim them if we took them by surprise. But that was risky, and if we failed, Mother might die.

At the hands of the anti-monarchists or by command of the throne.

"Pippa, help me think!" I hissed.

She crossed her arms and fixed her gaze on Carlina. "Think of how to help you free an anti-monarchist so you can hide her in your aunt's home where we are all staying?"

Realization flooded me. *Depths.* "I-I'm so sorry. I know what the anti-monarchists took from your people."

Pippa's jaw tightened. "No, you don't."

"I didn't want you naiads expelled," drawled Carlina. "If it eases your feelings."

"It doesn't," Pippa said curtly. "You are willing to align yourself with a violent mob. I do not particularly care to hear your reasoning."

Carlina shrugged. "Suit yourself."

Pippa was right. I shouldn't have brought her to court.

Not knowing Carlina was here and that I needed to free her. The guilt gnawed at me from the center of my chest.

"Pippa," I managed, my voice cracking—genuinely, this time. "When we're safe, I will owe you ten thousand apologies for so many things. This is one of the big ones. But I've met this mermaid before. And I really think that Mother is safer if we get Carlina out of here alive."

Pippa's gaze softened. "You *will* owe me ten thousand apologies. But I came here knowing what we had to do. I think we can get out up there." She gestured at the ceiling that allowed light and fresh water into the room through a narrow window covered by slatted bars.

I chewed the inside of my cheek. "You can get us through it?"

She peered up at it. "As long as there's enough time before the guards come in. I got us through a barred window while we were being poisoned in your home."

A flicker of genuine interest passed over Carlina's face. "Well, if I can avoid dying, I'm all for that."

Pippa ignored her and swam upward until she floated alongside the bars, examining the edges of the window. After running her hands along a couple of the bars, she swam back down, her mouth quirked.

"Problem?" I asked.

She nodded. "It's well-secured. No surprise, as any weaknesses could allow an intruder to breach the king's court."

"Can you get through it?"

"Yes. Of course." She glanced at the door. "But it will take a little time. I'm concerned they might get suspicious."

"Try," I said. "If you're willing to take that risk for us. Carlina and I will bar the door."

Carlina nodded, and I detected seriousness in her eyes somewhere beneath her layers of irony and apathy. She had to care, deeply. Why else would a leader of the anti-monarchists dedicate herself to restraining their worst impulses?

The thought comforted me. But not quite enough to make me feel entirely at ease about helping her escape.

Pippa swam upward, moving her hands in a small circle to conjure a globe of water. Stretching out her left hand, she sharpened the ball into a point just as she reached the window.

I hoped no guards would notice her from the outside.

My heart fluttered wildly as I turned to Carlina. She was already lugging the table from the far end of the room to set it against the door.

This is treason.

And there will be nowhere left for me to flee.

I shook my head. I'd figure that out later.

I lurched forward and grabbed two hammock chairs and dragged them toward the door, lifting them up above the floor just slightly so they wouldn't make a scraping sound.

Carlina finished positioning the table and swam past me back toward the center of the room.

"Will this be enough?" I asked her, pushing the chairs against the door.

She was already swimming back to the door, a chair in each arm. "No way to know without trying." She set the chairs down and fished a small blade, no longer than my forefinger, out of her wrap. "What? It's a netting blade," she said.

"I didn't say anything."

"I wasn't going to *stab* anyone with it. My own life isn't worth the risk that blood in the water would bring on the city." Her eyes met mine, and all the laissez-faire carelessness I'd seen in her earlier had vanished. "If I believed in saving my own fin above all other duties, I most certainly would not have joined a group of revolutionaries."

"I believe you."

She held my gaze for another pulsing of the gills and then turned her attention back to one of the chairs she'd just set down. "I'm going to strip the netting out of this, and we'll use it to help secure the door."

I nodded, glancing uneasily up at Pippa. *Abetting a fugitive* and *vandalism of the crown's property. We are definitely all going to die.*

Pippa was digging at the base of one of the bars with her water-spear. I hoped it would work. It had to. With a jerk of my head, I turned my attention back to Carlina. She was pulling the netting out of the base of the hammock chair.

"Here," she said when she'd gotten it free. "Take this. Thread it around the door handle two or three times."

I reached out and took it from her, staring at the netting woven together in interlocking loops. "Okay." I turned around, swam to the door, and hovered alongside it. My hands shook as I passed the loop of netting around the handle.

The table tilted upward, and I glanced underneath it to see Carlina pushing it up from the floor. She glanced from the door handle to one of the legs of the table, and I understood. As she pushed the table further upward, I took one of the empty loops of netting and threaded the table leg through it.

"Pull the table this way," said Carlina, grabbing one end and gesturing for me to take the other. We tugged the table away from the door until the rope was taut. Carlina cocked her head. "It won't hold them forever, but I think it should stop them from turning the handle at first. That should buy us time if they get—"

A booming knock sounded on the door. My heart caught in my throat.

Carlina shoved me. "Say something," she mouthed.

"Yes?" I called, hoping my voice didn't sound as nervous as I felt. I looked back up at Pippa. She'd gotten the two bars on the right side of the window free and was working on the third. We might be able to squeeze out once she had four free, but five would be better.

They'd come too soon.

"Lady Jade," came the deep voice. I presumed it to belong to a member of the Royal Mer Guard. "Is everything alright?"

"Yes! Great!"

Carlina shot me a look that meant murder.

"I need more time," I continued, lowering my pitch to a more somber tone. "Please. I just want to find my mother."

No reply came from the other side of the door. Perhaps he'd gone to report to Crown Prince Elias. I'd bought us time. I just didn't know how much.

My frantic gaze darted back up to Pippa, who had freed one end of the third bar and was digging at the other end. *One. Two. Three.* She jerked the bar out and dropped it, allowing it to sink to the floor alongside the first two.

Carlina and I exchanged a meaningful glance, and I saw that she was clenching her hands so hard that her fingertips had gone white.

I've just made a horrific mistake.

The knock sounded again.

"More time!" I cried. "I'm getting somewhere."

"Crown Prince Elias requests your immediate presence, Lady Jade. The traitor's, too."

"Just a moment. Please."

The doorknob jerked, almost imperceptibly, and I blanched. He'd tried the door. He knew we'd secured it. Which meant . . .

"Depths," he muttered. He slammed his hand against the door so hard I jumped. "Open this door immediately, by order of the crown prince."

I looked up at Pippa. She had just worked the first half of the fourth bar free. There wouldn't be time to get the fifth free. "Let's go," I whispered to Carlina, and we flicked our tails and surged upward toward Pippa.

"We're out of time," I said. "We have to go now."

Pippa didn't take her eyes off the bar. "Still working here."

I looked at the size of the gap. Not quite big enough. "They're coming."

With a grunt, she dug her spear into the base of the bar with vengeance, driving it cleanly through the bar. She drew back, staring at it, as if surprised. She dropped the bar and let it float to the ground.

"Let's go," I said. "Pippa first."

Pippa shook her head. "If the Guard comes, my water-casting is the only thing that stands between you and them."

My jaw tightened, but we didn't have time to argue. "Carlina, then."

"No arguments here," said Carlina, pushing her head and shoulders through the gap.

It occurred to me a moment too late that she might not wait for us.

A *thud* sounded against the door, as if a contingent of the Guard were trying to smash it in with a battering ram.

Carlina's hips caught in the gap, and my gills flared.

"Get out," I hissed.

Carlina tensed her muscle and surged forward, forcing herself through the window and into freedom. She whirled around, a grimace on her face.

This time, the *thud* shook the door.

"Now you, Jade," said Pippa.

I opened my mouth to protest, but we had no time. I launched toward the door, poked the top half of my body through and used my arms to pull myself out into the open water, just as a crashing sound came from inside the room. I pressed my face to the bars on the far side of the window.

Three soldiers spilled into the room through a hole in the door above the table and hammock chairs.

"Pippa!" I screamed.

Pippa was surging through the window now, pulling her way to freedom. I grabbed one of her hands to tug her the rest of the way, but one of the guards had grabbed her foot.

With a hiss, she wrested her hand free of mine and formed a ball of water that shimmered so brightly I had to squint to look at it. Turning her body, she threw it into the guard's face at the speed of a raging current. He fell backward, and she scrambled through the hole.

The three of us took off down the canal without another look behind.

The guards had all been muscled mermen. They wouldn't be able to fit through the hole after us. Which meant we just had to get away before they could leave through the main door of the king's court.

"Turn," I called as we approached the first intersecting canal.

"Where are we going?" Pippa asked, her voice shot through with tension.

The realization hit me. My mind raced. "I'm not sure. We can't go home. They'll look there."

I'm a fugitive. The words sounded strange, even in my head. And worst of all, I'd made Pippa a fugitive, too.

"The old naiad quarter," Pippa said. "I don't know if they'll look there, but they'd be hard-pressed to find us in the tunnels."

"The anti-monarchists are there." I hazarded a glance at Carlina. She didn't react.

"All the better," said Pippa. "I think you've just earned the right to collect your mother from their custody."

*C*arlina, Pippa, and I slipped into the tunnels at the end of Pippa's old canal, glancing around us to make sure we weren't noticed. This part of the city still felt deserted. And if any anti-monarchists were watching through the windows, well . . . they certainly weren't about to turn us in to the Royal Mer Guard.

"What was that?" I asked Pippa as she fastened the trapdoor above us.

"What was what?" Her eyes were hard.

"That . . . light . . . thing?"

She didn't react. "I don't know."

"How did you do it?"

"I needed to."

"Why . . . " I couldn't finish the question.

"Why didn't I fight like that while my people were being slaughtered in the canals?"

I pursed my lips. "I didn't mean it like that."

Her voice took on a monotonous quality. "I've already told you that we could have taken the city if we'd organized and fought back."

"But when the Guard came . . . "

"I'd have just died, too!" she cried. "They were killing any naiads they found in the canals. Best way to stop it was to get the depths off the canals! We had no time. Not enough warning. I . . . "

"It's okay." I reached out to touch her arm, but she shook me off.

"Of course, I knew some naiads might die," she said. "In my head, I knew it. But . . . the rabble-rousers. The ones who fought back. Not so many. Not"—her voice caught—"children."

We said nothing, and then she continued, "Of course I would have fought if I'd known. Do you think that I don't live with that every day? Do you think I'll forget it for one single moment for the rest of my life?"

"I wasn't blaming you," I said.

"I was."

I fell silent, and Carlina broke the awkward tension. "Well. If I—"

"It should have been you," Pippa said.

Carlina glanced between Pippa and me uneasily. "What now?"

Pippa was shaking now. "The king sent the Guard after us because it was easier. To send a message. To still the unrest in the city. But you revolutionaries were the ones causing the instability. Fomenting the violence. It was you the king wanted to send the Guard after. But it would have been too politically unpopular. Nobles would have defended you. Working-class mer might have taken up arms alongside you.

"No one cared about us. It should have been you skubs who were dragged out into the canals to be slaughtered." She darted forward and shoved Carlina up against the wall of the tunnel.

Carlina cast a desperate look at me, but I wasn't going to get in the middle of this. Not when every word Pippa had said was true. Not after she'd lost so much.

Mustering her bravado, Carlina scoffed. "So, what? You going to kill me after that whole spectacle back there where you stole me from the crown prince's custody?"

"I'm one of the last naiads still here in the city." Pippa's voice dropped low and harsh. "So, I'd say you owe me a blood debt. You owe one to Jade, here, too, because your little social club murdered her father."

"Before my time in—"

"Save it." Pippa released Carlina and took a step backward.

Carlina smoothed her ruffled wrap. "You want Cleo. As if that would wipe out every wrong we've done in service of our ideals."

"Not even close," said Pippa. "And I won't bluff and threaten to kill you. It's not my way, and you don't strike me as the sort of mer who would sell out her ideals, no matter the cost. That's why you've tolerated so much collateral damage."

"I don't believe the consequences of an action have much bearing on whether it's the morally right thing to do, no."

"And you value doing the morally correct thing," I said, "more than anything."

Carlina studied her fingernails. "My code of morality is not one you noble merchildren would recognize, but I act with integrity and consistency in my life."

"And does kidnapping my mother fit neatly in with that code of *morality*?"

She tilted her chin up toward us. "Thank you for rescuing me. I think I'll be on my way now."

Pippa opened her fists and ten tiny water-spears materialized, darting to take their places a mere hands-breadth from Carlina's head, encircling her scalp. "You'll stay here for a bit longer," said Pippa, her voice frigid.

The tips of the water-spears looked as sharp as blades, and I floated forward to place my hand on Pippa's shoulder. "Maybe we should think about this," I said.

"Don't get me started on you," she said. "I love you like a sister, but you've done so many things so terribly since your fiancé killed my actual sister."

"Ex-fiancé," I muttered.

"Not at the time."

"Have you snapped?" I demanded.

"Just tired of putting up with all the idiot mer in this city," she quipped.

At least this time she shot a wink at me. Perhaps that was a good sign.

"Listen." Pippa turned her attention back to Carlina. "If we let you go back right now, there are good odds that Lady Cleo dies. And if she does, her blood will bring the sharks to your door."

"Can you offer anything in negotiation for Cleo's release?"

"You sleeping better at night?" I offered. "Or, retroactively, being rescued from the crown prince?"

Carlina's nose twitched, and her expression changed. "Tell you what. I'll do it."

I opened my mouth and then closed it.

"Come again?" asked Pippa.

"I'll bring Cleo back to you here on one condition."

"And what condition is that?"

"That you arrange a private audience for me with that harpy senator from Marbella."

"You want a meeting with Senator Ti?" I asked slowly.

"Is that so hard to believe?"

Pippa and I exchanged a long look.

"Fine," Carlina spat. "I don't think Faustus should have taken your brother, and I argued with him when he exchanged the kid for Cleo. I'll help you get her back. But I also want to meet with the senator."

"You do realize she's a harpy?" I asked, my eyes tapering.

"I do believe I just said that, yes."

"And with the bigotry the anti-monarchists have displayed toward naiads, you expect me to believe that you have a genuine desire to meet with a harpy?"

"Why not?" She smirked, as if knowing she'd asked a question I couldn't comfortably answer.

I deflected. "Senator Ti has hardly been seen in public since her arrival because anti-harpy sentiment runs deep among the mer here."

Pippa crossed her arms. "Didn't you already meet with the senator?"

She was right. Ti had met with Faustus . . . I'd forgotten.

"Faustus did," said Carlina. "I was . . . taking care of a disciplinary matter."

"You were executing George's murderer."

"Oh, I didn't do it myself," she said. "But yes, I want to meet the senator. And no, I don't care that she's harpy. As I said before, I had nothing against the naiads personally—"

Pippa grunted.

"I just want to learn more about what democracy looks like in the real world, you know. I believe in it. I absolutely believe in it. But it's been theoretical my whole life. I grew up here, with stuffy nobles looking down on us regular folk and a tyrant ruling on the throne."

I let the jab pass. It was probably true, after all.

"The senator can tell me firsthand how democracy really works. We can use that information to implement it here, piece by piece. The princeling won't give us a senate, not at first, but we can work toward more and more self-rule with every compromise he makes. And we can do that better if we have a real senator from a real democracy advising us."

Ti was as likely to upbraid Carlina as to advise her. But I'd sort of like to see that.

"No private meeting," I said. "For the senator's security. I'm sure we can arrange a meeting for you. But the senator must consent to it. She is already aware of the methods the Thessaloniken anti-monarchists have used to oppose the crown."

Carlina nodded. "I'll agree to those terms. Now . . . " She glanced at the water-spears still pointed at her head. "Get rid of those, will you?"

Pippa tightened her hands back into fists, and the spears evaporated, rejoining the shapeless water.

Carlina glanced down the tunnel. "If I follow that, will I reach the tunnels under . . . Camford Canal, I think it used to be called?"

"It will intersect," said Pippa.

"I'll be back with Cleo." Carlina held my gaze. "As soon as I can. Sometime tonight when it's dark."

"How can I know that?" I asked.

"Do you have any other choice besides trusting me?"

"Is lying in opposition to your moral code?"

"Not always." Something like a smile ghosted the corners of her lips. "But lying about this would be."

I wanted to point out that we couldn't know whether she was lying about *that*, but she was right. We had to trust that she'd bring Mother back.

And hope she wouldn't bring a gang of anti-monarchists with her.

SEVENTEEN

Pippa and I sat on the seafloor in the gathering gloom, a markedly awkward silence resting between us. I rubbed my hands over my feathery fin, hoping the familiar texture would help me focus on the here-and-now and not the *what-if*s spinning wildly through my head.

I was the first to break the tension. "You wouldn't really have hurt her, would you have?"

The expression on her heart-shaped face didn't change. "Not too badly."

"Did you mean everything you said?"

She turned to look at me, as if surprised. "Of course. Every word."

"I'm sorry I've been so terrible."

"You've gotten better. Really, you have. Or maybe you were just out of town so long that I actually started to miss your face."

She smiled, but the words still stung. Her face softened, and she reached over and grabbed my hand. "I don't blame you for any of it, you know. Not really. You're trying to be better, and that's why I can count you as a sister. There's a lot you're unlearning, and that takes time. Not something we've had much of. Everything's been moving fast for you."

"You're kinder than I deserve."

"That's what friends are for."

There was another long pause, and then I asked, "Will you stay here, do you think?"

"In Thessalonike? I think I lost that choice when I helped you free Carlina."

A throbbing sadness bloomed in my chest. "I'm so sorry."

"I'm not. I ache for the rivers. I've felt it for a long time, but it's more acute now that my people are gone. Now that they're in a far-off city, under the rule of a foreign invader. I don't know what it's like for them in Marbella, now. I hope better than it was here.

"But my place isn't in the ocean anymore. It never has been, really. As soon as Lady Cleo is back and safe, I'm going to strike out for the coast. Swim alongside it until I happen upon a river system that's still thriving. Find naiads who will let me stay."

"You think you'll find that?"

She laughed a little. "Yes. Since it's just me. If it were the whole community, I doubt it. But alone, I think I can find a friendly river."

"Tides keep you safe."

"I hope so."

She shifted closer to me and put her arm around my shoulder. I leaned against her, sorrow and joy brimming inside me. I felt in my marrow that she would find the safe harbor she sought. That her story would go on for a long time in happiness and peace. She deserved that. But, depths, I would miss her.

⌒

We waited in the tunnels for a long time, enjoying each other's company in the quiet depths of the seafloor. I tried to relish each moment, recognizing they were some of the last I would spend in her company.

"They'll be watching for you at the city wall," I said. "You'll need to be careful leaving the city."

"I've thought of that. I'll time it for the crown prince's coronation, I think, in a few days. The Guard will be on high alert at the center of the city. They'll have fewer soldiers stationed on the walls. I'll find a quiet section, lightly patrolled, and try to slip out unnoticed. If they give chase, I'll have the advantage of speed, and I'm not afraid of open water."

I wanted to ask her to stay longer, but I held it in. It was selfish to ask her to put herself in danger a moment longer than necessary. To ask her to risk being here when the Neptunians swept through. I wouldn't do that.

She glanced up at the crack around the trapdoor, which let in a thin curtain of light. "I think it's starting to get dark. It should be low tide soon. Hopefully, Carlina and Cleo won't be too far behind."

I hoped Benjamin wasn't too worried. Alexander wouldn't realize I was missing. He wouldn't have any reason to think I hadn't gone home. But to see the look on Benjamin's face when I brought Mother back . . .

Except I couldn't go back home. Or to see Alexander the next day. Because the Guard would be looking for me.

I pressed my lips together. Mother wouldn't be pleased that I'd made myself a criminal to save her. But that's what she'd done for Benjamin. Though the crown prince had no proof that she'd turned herself over to the anti-monarchists on purpose.

We'll figure out the rest later. I repeated it in my head over and over.

If Mother didn't kill me herself when she found out what I'd done.

But something in me couldn't shake what I felt to be true: That saving Carlina had been the right thing to do, regardless of the consequences. I didn't trust Elias to give her a fair trial. I wasn't convinced that a monarch should have rule of the city. It would have been wrong to float by and let her die. To let Elias murder her like King Stephanos had murdered Andronicus.

Depths. I'm becoming one of them.

It had been happening almost imperceptibly—first when the Guard massacred the naiads. A bit more when the king wanted to use Yvonna's death to help himself consolidate power. When I saw democracy at work in Marbella. When I went to the play starring Claira Aliza about the princess who fell in love with a revolutionary. And then when the king died and his inept son rose to the throne.

No, I hadn't joined the anti-monarchists' organization—because I despised their methods. But I'd become one of them in the most secret part of my heart. I hoped they would get their senate, if the Neptunians didn't enslave us all.

As though Pippa could sense my thoughts, she said, "The world is changing, Jade. It's alright to change with it."

"You sound tired."

"I am. So are you."

"I just don't know what I'm fighting anymore."

"Then don't fight."

I leaned back to study her face in the dim light. "What do you mean? What are any of us doing, then?"

"I don't know. But I'm not sure fighting the evil ever does as much as protecting the good. And that's why we're here right now. To save Cleo."

The murmuring of quiet voices caused my head to jerk to the right. Could it be? Already? Or had the anti-monarchists come to collect us?

I squeezed Pippa's hand until I couldn't feel my fingers.

The voices grew closer, taking on timbre and resonance. I knew those voices.

My chin trembled. "Mother!" I cried, pushing myself off the sand and darting down the dark tunnel.

EIGHTEEN

"Jade!" Mother wrapped her arms around me, enveloping me in a tight embrace. "Benjamin? Is he home? Is he safe?"

"He's safe, Mother. He's safe. We're all safe."

She pulled back and looked me in the eyes. "Carlina told me what you did. You know I absolutely disapprove."

But warmth glimmered in her face, just discernible in the murky water.

She pulled me back into a hug. "What am I supposed to do with you, child?"

"Keep me under lock and key, I suppose," I said, my voice husky.

"You'd still find ways to get into trouble."

"So would you."

"Lady Cleo," said Pippa from behind us. "I'm very glad you're safe. Hi, Maximus."

I glanced up, startled, and realized that Maximus had come down the tunnel with Mother and Carlina. "Thank you," I mouthed at him. My stomach ached. I'd have to give him the news about Orua.

"Pippa!" Mother moved away from me and swam toward Pippa, her arms outstretched. "We don't deserve you."

Pippa tensed as Mother pulled her into a hug, but slowly, uncertainly, put her arms around her in return.

I cast a quizzical glance in their direction and then looked at Carlina. Mother was not given to outward displays of affection, even to her children. *Odd* . . .

"Are you hurt, Mother? Did they torture you?"

"No, actually." She released Pippa. "Not physically, anyway."

I was about to ask what *not physically* meant when a shudder ran through her body.

"I don't want to talk about it. Not yet."

I shot Carlina a murderous look, but she was gazing studiously at the wall of the tunnel.

Mother crossed her arms. "I suppose you can't go home, Jade and Pippa."

I shook my head. "Not after crossing Elias like that."

Mother glanced toward the trickle of light just barely filtering in from the nearest trapdoor. "You can't stay here, either."

"Well I can't very well sneak through the city. Even with a cloak I wouldn't blend in. Not right now, when most mer are avoiding the canals."

"And I'd stand out like a jellyfish," said Pippa.

"I'll take them to an abandoned house," said Carlina. "There are a number of us in this part of the city, but I know some safe dwellings. They can stay in one of those until it's safe for them to return."

"But how long will that be?" asked Mother, her voice grim.

I gazed down at the floor. If Elias stayed in power . . . never.

Even if he openly forgave me, I'd defied him. Embarrassed him in his own court. There would be no more *safe* for me in Thessalonike while he ruled.

If I were to regain any semblance of a life here, it would only be because the anti-monarchists succeeded in unseating Elias. Whether Theo took the throne or the anti-monarchists managed to implement their long-dreamed-of democracy didn't matter. But Elias and I could not coexist in the same city.

I hazarded a glance at Mother, and something passed between us—the knowledge, perhaps, that nothing could ever be the same again. That we'd both crossed a drop-off and begun treading water above a bottomless chasm.

And now Mother had to entrust her oldest child to a revolutionary leader.

"Maximus can go home now, of course," said Carlina. "I don't know how sympathetic to us you really are, Max, but I know you came because Jade asked you to."

He and I looked at each other. I guess we hadn't been that sneaky.

"You won't tell Faustus or any of the others where they are?" Mother asked.

"No," said Carlina. "There's no reason for Faustus to know, and . . . I owe Pippa a debt."

Pippa tilted her head. "You brought Cleo back already."

Carlina's voice softened. "That was my debt to Jade."

"Go to Benjamin, Mother. He needs you. I'll be alright. I made my choice."

"And I will always be angry at you for that." But there was no anger in her voice, just a deep sense of exhaustion. Mother had always been tightly controlled—even controlling, in her worst moments. But now we faced an impending reality that none of us could control. Not really. We could only go day by day and hope we lived to see the next high tide.

"I'll see that she gets home safely," said Maximus, his voice husky.

"Wait. I . . . have something to tell you."

"What?" His eyes searched mine, and concern filled his face. "What's wrong?"

"It's Orua. She's in the house of healing. She's injured."

Even in the dim light, I thought I saw the color drain from his face. "How badly?"

I shifted. "I don't know. She was speared . . . "

Maximus whirled on Carlina. "Did you do this? Did your mer hurt her?"

Carlina backed away from him. "I swear to you I know nothing of this. If the anti-monarchists attacked a member of the Guard, Faustus told me nothing of it.'"

Mother rested her hand on my shoulder. "Will she be alright?"

"The physicians said to not lose hope," I managed weakly.

Maximus groaned, a deep, guttural sound that spoke of intense pain.

"Go to her now, Maximus," said Mother. "I'll be alright getting home."

Without another word, Maximus surged down the tunnel to the trapdoor, and broke out onto the canal above.

Mother squeezed my hand and then turned and swam for the trapdoor where Maximus had disappeared.

My stomach hurt. I watched her go, and when she'd disappeared into the canal above us, I turned to Carlina. "Where are we going?"

Carlina gestured to the bare walls around us. "You'll be safe here."

Pippa turned her head left and right, inspecting the interior of the hovel. "This will do very well," she said. She glanced at me, her eyebrows arched. "It is much like the house where I used to live with Anna. Jade may need some time to get used to it."

"No," I said. "I love it. It's perfect."

Pippa was right that it was different from where I'd grown up, but I was just happy to have a safe place to sleep for the night.

Besides, I'd long complained that the nobles were wealthy to excess. It was time I started living like I meant it. Perhaps Alexander and I would settle down in a place like this. Forget fancy careers and all the nobles, and do honest work with our hands. I'd never settled on a career I wanted to pursue. No particular kind of work had captured my imagination. I just wanted to do work that *meant* something.

That would be a good life.

"Where will you go, Carlina?" I turned to look at the blue-haired mermaid. "You said that the Guard came for you at home."

She shrugged. "I thought maybe I'd stay here with you. Keeps everyone safer, I suspect. That alright?"

"I'm glad to hear it," I said. I glanced around the barren house again. "Any way that you can get us three hammocks from your revolutionary friends?"

Carlina quirked her mouth. "Does the spoiled noble think that hammocks rise up fully formed out of the coral?"

"I . . ."

Pippa tried unsuccessfully to hide a smirk behind her hand.

"Okay, then. Cloaks to lie on." I didn't bother to suppress my flash of irritation at her mockery.

"Aye," said Carlina. "I think I can find us three cloaks to spread out on the sand. I'll use the tunnels and be back before high tide."

Pippa quirked her mouth. "You don't think they'll be suspicious? Surely, word has spread through the canals that you escaped the king's court with a noble and a naiad? What if they figure out you're harboring us?"

"Trust me," said Carlina. "I won't let on. I'll be back soon."

With her hand held up as if to preempt any more argument, she swam to the trapdoor in the back of the house and jerked it open. A moment later, she'd disappeared, replacing the trapdoor carefully behind her.

Pippa and I were alone.

"Do you think Mother will tell Alexander what's happened?" I asked. "He'll be worried when I'm not there tomorrow."

"Benjamin will make sure of it," she said. "He's almost grown-up, and he adores Alexander. He'll remember."

"We didn't even devise a way to send messages back and forth," I said, pacing to the door of the house and back again. "How could we have left out something so elementary?"

"Carlina has resources," said Pippa. "And so does your mother. Besides, every day the canals are busier, bit by bit. People can't stay indoors, afraid, forever. If we need to slip through the crowd, we'll be able to. Not tomorrow or the day after, but soon."

"You're right." My anxious temperament was getting the best of me. I sank to the floor and dug my hands into the sand, hoping the rough, familiar texture would calm me. I closed my eyes. "Tell me facts, Pippa. Four or five of them. Not related to anything we're afraid of."

"Just . . . facts?"

I opened one eye to peer at her, and she was regarding me skeptically, her arms crossed.

"Yes. Anything. Just things that everyone knows are true."

"Um . . . if you drop a heavy object, it sinks to the seafloor. Like that?"

"Yes." I dropped my head into my arms. "I'm trying to stay sane."

"Okay."

I felt her hand rest tentatively on my shoulder.

"The sun never dips below the surface. Kiki is a gray dolphin."

"All bottlenose dolphins are gray," I said without lifting my head.

"There you go. Your fourth fact."

"What's the fifth?"

Her hand slid across my back until her arm was wrapped around my shoulder. "Benjamin and Cleo are safe."

Something broke inside me, and my chin quivered. "They're safe."

"Oh, are you going to cry again?" she asked, a teasing tone in her voice.

"Probably."

"Why?"

"I don't know the surface from the seafloor anymore. Everything's happened so fast, and the world is changing, and I'm changing, and so is everyone I love."

A knock sounded on the trapdoor.

I furrowed my brow. "She's back already?"

Pippa shrugged. "Maybe she forgot something."

The knock came again. "Why isn't she just coming in?" I snapped, exasperated.

A half-formed thought tugged at the back of my mind as I swam to the door, but I shook it aside. It had to be Carlina. Who else knew we were here?

I yanked the trapdoor opened and shot upward with a cry. Tor's face peered up at me.

NINETEEN

"What the depths?" Tor clutched the edge of the trap-door, his knuckles white.

Fear jolted through me.

"Why are you here?" he and I asked in unison.

I backed away from him, my eyes searching the house for anything I could use to defend myself. I settled on a rock the size of my fist that sat next to the trapdoor—probably to weigh it down—and darted forward to wrest it into my hands.

Pippa jetted up next to me, her hands held back, ready to cast water.

Tor put his hands up, palms facing us. "Hey, hey, hey. I'm sorry. I didn't know you were here."

We stared at each other in tense silence.

"So. Why. Are. *You*. Here?" I asked through gritted teeth.

He clutched the edge of the opening. "I suspect we have a lot to catch up on. Can I come in?"

I glanced at Pippa and then back at Tor. "Not sure you want to do that."

Pippa sputtered. "What gives you the right to think I want to be in the same room as you?"

Tor held her gaze. "There's no reason you should want to be in the same room as me. And that's to my great shame."

Pippa's gaze remained steely, but she stepped backward. "I'll defer to Jade."

I hesitated. I didn't believe Tor was a physical danger to us. At least not of his own volition. He'd saved my life on the journey to Marbella and hadn't moved a finger to harm me at any point during that journey. And I didn't see any reason why he'd want to hurt Pippa.

But who knew who might have sent him. Tor might not have intrinsic motivation to do me harm anymore, but I wasn't under any illusions that he was above acting under threat or bribe.

"First, tell me why you're here," I said. "Did you follow us?"

His eyebrows rose almost all the way to his hairline. "I'd think it should be pretty clear that I didn't, since I was as surprised to see you here as you were to see me."

I bit my lip in exasperation. "Just tell me why you're here."

"I've been staying here for days. Since I returned."

Pippa and I glanced at each other, and then I looked back at Tor, focusing on his face to try to figure out whether he was lying.

"Why?" Pippa asked, incredulous.

"Because I'm not very well going to return to my father's house, and too many mer in this city will find their lives easier if I'm dead."

Chewing a fingernail, I floated backward. "Come in. But don't think you're staying the night."

"Wouldn't dream of it after finding you here," he muttered. "I do have some sense of self-preservation."

"I'm pretty sure I had a chance to kill you before and didn't take it," I retorted.

He winced. "That was the second-most horrific thing I've ever done. Not a night I want to dwell on."

"Sit down." I gestured to the sandy floor. "It isn't much, but I suppose you know that if you've been staying here."

Tor unclasped a long black cloak from around his shoulders, folded it in half twice, and set it on an undisturbed patch of sand. He rubbed the shadow of a beard on his chin—a new addition that didn't improve his appearance, not that my opinion mattered anymore—and sank down onto the cloak.

I hovered a tail-length in front of him and faced him, sinking down to the floor. "Who wants you dead?"

He traced a circle in the sand in front of him. "My father, for one. But he's not the one I'm particularly worried about. That honor belongs to Elias, I'm afraid."

That piqued my curiosity. "What does Elias want with you?"

He gazed at the wall. "I may have disobeyed a direct order. Besides, he always hated me in school, the little shrimp."

"Anyone else?"

"I think I've infuriated an anti-monarchist or two recently."

"Any in particular?"

"I'm not Faustus's favorite."

"We have so much in common."

"I guess I don't need to ask you how you managed that."

"Seems like opposing you publicly was reason enough." I pressed my fingertips together. "I thought the anti-monarchists liked you."

"Well, now Faustus hates both of us."

"Care to share why?"

"Not particularly, but suffice it to say that it's because I won't be a pawn in his game. He wanted to use Father's trade connections to advance his own agenda, but I'm done helping my father make and keep allies."

"Why?" Pippa asked.

"My *father* killed my mother!" spat Tor. "And I know I'm partially to blame for how everything fell apart, and I know that you of all people should have no sympathy for my grief, but he . . . he destroyed everything I'd sacrificed my soul to protect."

I glanced at Pippa but couldn't quite read her expression. But I was quite sure that Tor was correct, that she had little—if any—sympathy for him.

I didn't blame her. Tor didn't either, from the tortured expression on his face. Was it too much to hope that someone could change so dramatically in so short a period of time? Was I naive to draw any other conclusion than that he was playing the changing tides in his own self-interest? Or maybe he did feel real grief, but it was the sort of passing emotion that would fade by the end of storm season.

"Well," Pippa said, taking a step forward and kneeling down, reaching out her hands to clasp his. "I'm very sorry for your loss."

My gills flared sharply.

"Thank you," said Tor in a strangled voice. "I'd give anything to take back what I did to your sister."

Pippa's hands were trembling now. "Me too."

I felt awkward, like I didn't belong here in this room, witnessing this moment.

"Anna deserved justice," said Pippa. "But she never liked vengeance. There's very little in me that wants to extend forgiveness to you, especially when I think of who I've lost. But when I *really* think about her—about who she was and what she would have wanted—I know that I must. If you're sincere. That doesn't mean I'll ever really trust you. But at the very least, know that I don't wish you harm. Even if the sentence the king handed down was far lighter than you deserved."

"I acknowledge that," he said, his voice husky. "And thank you for being more gracious than you needed to be."

Pippa responded with a slight nod and moved back, putting distance between them.

Tor rubbed his temples and looked over at me. "So, who are you on the run from?"

"Primarily, Elias," I said. "I also disobeyed a direct order. Helped an anti-monarchist escape."

He jerked his head up. "Why—"

The scraping of the trapdoor interrupted us. The wooden frame lifted upward, and a familiar teal-haired mermaid swam in, carrying an armful of cloaks.

"You would not believe my luck," Carlina chirped. She pulled up short when she saw the three of us. "Oh! I see Tor made it here earlier than I expected."

"You knew he was coming?" I demanded.

Carlina swam closer and handed me two cloaks. "Well, I thought I'd have a chance to talk to you about it first, but yes."

"What the depths, Carlina?" Tor jolted upward. "What were you thinking, bringing them here?"

She handed two cloaks to Pippa and set two more down on the sand. "That we can all help each other out."

"I don't need Tor's help. I don't care if he's reformed himself, and I don't care that he saved my life on the way to Marbella. I mean"—I glanced over at Tor—"I *am* grateful for that. But it doesn't change the reality that there is far too much baggage there. I can wish him well, but we need to go our separate ways."

"I agree," said Tor, again tracing shapes in the sand. "We can't unsink that ship."

"Would you just listen to me?" asked Carlina, exasperation lacing her voice.

Tor, Pippa, and I all exchanged glances among ourselves.

"I'll listen," Pippa offered.

Tor and I shrugged in reply.

Carlina hovered just above the floor. "The four of us are here in this room together because we all will benefit from the completion of a very specific task."

"What's that?" Pippa asked, her arms folded.

"The assassination of Elias."

TWENTY

"**D**epths, no," I said. "What kind of mer do you think I am?"

"I took you for having a good survival instinct." Carlina picked at one of her fingernails. "Was I wrong?"

"What do you think? I made myself a fugitive to save your life."

"That was primarily to save your mother's life," said Carlina, "but your point is taken."

I looked at Tor and Pippa for backup and was relieved to see them shaking their heads.

"I told you, Carlina," Tor said in a low voice. "I'm done with all that."

Her expression softened, and I glanced between them. *Were they . . .* I let the thought trail off. Tor's personal life wasn't my business.

"I'm out, too," said Pippa. "I'm not going to make myself a murderer."

Tor winced.

Carlina sank back down onto the sand. "You'd rather let the whole city fall than kill one merman? A merman who deserves to die? Jade, he would have let your brother die before he even hinted at a compromise with the anti-monarchists."

"And why was my brother in danger in the first place?" I spat. "Because your goons killed George, who was like a second father to me, and kidnapped Benjamin."

A flash of annoyance crossed her face. "I already told you, I executed the merman who killed your butler, and Benjamin was never in any real danger."

"And how can I believe that he wasn't? When the anti-monarchists have left so much devastation in their wake?"

"Our collateral damage pales in comparison to the destruction done by the Royal Mer Guard."

"I wasn't aware this was a competition just to be *less bad* than other mer."

"Could you just—"

"Stop!" Tor raised his hands. "I won't participate in this, Carlina, and that's final. And I don't appreciate how you've gone about any of this."

"Your mother would have supported this. She always was sympathetic to our cause."

"Don't tell me what my mother would have done."

I glanced between them. This didn't seem like a romance. It suddenly seemed like . . .

"I loved her, too, you know," she said.

"You barely knew her."

"She was always kind to me. She remembered where she came from. She loved her sister, and she loved me."

Tor raked his fingers through his hair. "I appreciate the—"

"Wait . . . " I said.

"Tor's my cousin." Carlina glanced at us. "His mother married up. Mine married a laborer. Their children had different opportunities."

I had so many questions. So. Many. Questions.

Pippa broke the tension. "What a surprise that two of my least favorite people are related to each other," she quipped. Then her face grew serious. "Maybe Elias does deserve to die."

The words sent quillpricks down my spine. It was treason even to say it.

"But that doesn't mean we should stoop to his level. If we

join a plot to kill him, how are we any less murderous than he is?"

"Listen," Carlina said. "Jade herself brought news that the Neptunians are coming. We don't know when, but we can assume they'll be here soon. Do you think Elias has any chance of standing up to them? He lacks both the steady temperament and wisdom of the ancient monarchs in the old stories. We'll be conquered."

My eyes narrowed. "Not two days ago, you argued that it might be better to be conquered than to continue to live under the Thessaloniken monarchy. You change your story whenever it suits your own ends."

"I have been known to do that," said Carlina, holding my gaze. "But actually, I'm quite serious. You made me think. I don't want foreign rulers on the throne any more than I want Elias to wear the crown. And conveniently, the best way to prevent both of those things is to take out Elias."

"Theo will assume the throne, then. You'll still have a monarchy. The whole social order cannot change so quickly. Not in time for the city to unite around a democracy before the Neptunians get here."

"I know," said Carlina. "Which is why I've come to support the idea of Prince Theo taking the throne in place of Elias. At least for now."

Pippa did a double-take. "You, an anti-monarchist leader, are supporting the next-in-line to the throne?"

"Theo is reasonable in ways that Elias is not. I can tolerate Thessalonike remaining technically a monarchy if the new king is willing to grant us some degree of self-rule. Elias will do no such thing. He's made his colors clear. But Theo? Word in the canals is that he's more stable. That he even suggested the compromise of a democratically-elected advisory body. I'm not enthusiastic about any king, but I'll tolerate one like that if I have to. And, right now, I'm pretty sure I have to."

I pressed my fingernails into my palms to sharpen my focus. "Why are you bringing this to us? Why not to your anti-monarchist friends, who have already shown themselves willing to commit treason?"

"Well, so have you," Carlina said with a sardonic smile. "You defied the crown prince in his own court. But, of course, I brought it to you because Faustus and his ilk are not likely to appreciate statements like, 'I'll tolerate a king if I have to.'"

"And we're not likely to appreciate statements like, 'Let's stage an assassination,'" I said. "Have Cassian do it."

Pippa snapped her fingers. "But what if the core idea wasn't crazy?"

Carlina glared at her. "It's not crazy."

Pippa ignored her. "I'm serious. None of us is willing to assist in a plan to kill Elias, of course, but what if we helped push the balance of power over to Theo? Would he take control, do you think, if given the chance?"

I looked up at the ceiling, squinting. "I . . . I don't think so. He's loyal. It would have to be a pretty significant impetus."

"Like the fact that the city will fall to the Neptunians if he doesn't?" asked Pippa.

"Maybe . . . " But I doubted it.

Tor shook his head. "What if it just destabilizes everything further, right at the point the Neptunians arrive?"

"The longer we delay, the more likely that outcome becomes," said Carlina.

"We should talk to Ti," I said with a sudden flash of clarity.

Carlina smirked. "Now we're talking. I told you I wanted an audience with her."

"Well, we can't very well bring her here," said Pippa. "A harpy in the canals will draw more attention than three fugitives and a naiad."

"Four fugitives," said Carlina. "One of whom is a naiad."

Pippa held up her hands as if conceding the point.

"So, what exactly does that mean?" Tor asked slowly.

But he already knew the answer. We all did.

"It means we have to creep through the canals under cover of darkness," I said. "And hope we don't get arrested for treason."

CHAPTER

TWENTY-ONE

"*The plan is simple.* I repeated it over and over in my head. Sneak to Aunt Junia's recently fortified house. Break in through the back door or a window, to avoid tipping off the guards who were providing Aunt Junia security. And somehow have a conversation with Ti about her thoughts on overthrowing the foreign government currently sheltering her.

Easy as crabcakes.

Of all the bad decisions I'd made in recent months, this had to be one of my most foolhardy. Or perhaps my second-most foolhardy. Rescuing a fugitive from under the nose of the crown prince still arguably took first place.

The tunnel was quiet as we wrapped our cloaks tightly around our heads, hoping they would keep us unnoticed, or at least unrecognized.

Pippa stretched out her hands and shaped a little current of water into a mer fin and tail. It was translucent and didn't move quite like a real tail, but it might fool someone looking on from a distance in the dark.

Carlina shifted the trapdoor and moved up onto the canal first. After a long, terrifying moment, she called in a low voice, "Looks clear to me. Let's go."

One by one, we swam upward, and then Tor and I replaced the trapdoor.

With silent nods at each other, we began swimming—

146

slowly, so that Pippa could keep her focus on maintaining the shape of the mer tail.

Down another canal. Out of the old naiad quarter. Toward Aunt Junia's home.

Startled, I realized we were going to pass the garden of statues in the center of the city. The statues of the ancients, that told the stories of Thessalonike. Not even Tor knew how much these works of art meant to me. No one did except Mother and Aunt Junia.

When we reached the end of long, narrow canal we'd taken, we emerged on the edge of the grouping of statues, row after row of them silhouetted in the dim light.

"Swim straight through," I said in a low voice. "We're less likely to be noticed in the midst of them than in the open part of the square."

I took the lead, choosing the row that contained my two favorite statues—my ancestors, the warrior queen Eliana and my namesake, Queen Jade, who showed mercy that cost her life.

We couldn't linger, but I reached out a hand to brush the stone hands as we passed by, hoping to find in myself some measure of their strength and dignity.

I hazarded a glance up at Queen Jade. Her features were different from mine, but I'd always felt a deep connection with her. Mother and Father had given me the name *Jade* for a reason. Maybe some part of me felt that I needed to live up to my namesake to fulfill their expectations. But that was silly. I wanted to be like Jade because she'd been a good person, willing to sacrifice herself for the benefit of others. Conscious of her own impact on the world around her.

Raising my chin, I surged forward, just a little faster.

We slipped down a side canal. Now we were in the part of the city that I knew so well, and relief tugged at my heart. I could get us home unnoticed from here. I was sure of it.

Four turns later, we approached the back of Aunt Junia's

house. I held up a hand to signal the others to stop two tail-lengths away, and I floated forward to peek in the two windows that faced the back alley. The first room—the kitchen—was mostly blocked by closed shutters, but when I peered through the crack along the bottom of the second window, I made out a hammock bed against the far wall and a desk just underneath the window. We could probably pry the shutters off, but the noise might alert the guards.

Then I detected movement inside. My heart hammered, and I floated downward as quietly as I could. I needed to figure out who was inside that room without being seen. A flash of short blue hair passed by the crack between the two shutters.

Benjamin.

"Urchin," I whispered as loudly as I dared. I hazarded a slight tap on the shutters. "It's me. Open up."

Benjamin's eye appeared in the hairline opening. "Jade?" he squeaked.

"Shh!" I hissed. "Open the window."

His shadow backed away from the window, and after a long pause, I heard a soft scraping sound and the shutters swung open. He leaned out and gave me a hug. "What are you doing here?" he whispered. "It isn't safe. The Guard is still out front."

"I know," I said, "but we needed to talk to the senator."

"We?"

I gestured the others forward with my hand.

"Can you get Ti in here without causing a stir?" I asked.

Pippa came up alongside me, and Benjamin's eyes widened as he looked behind us at Tor and Carlina.

"*What* is going on?" he whispered.

"I'll explain it all later if I can," I said. "Right now, there are things you're safer not knowing. That way you can answer honestly if they question you. Just please bring Ti in here."

"I'll do my best," he said. "Get in here. You shouldn't be in the canals. *Everyone* is looking for you."

"Tell me something I don't know," I murmured. I swam upward and through his window, followed first by Pippa and then Tor and Carlina.

"Wait," I said, setting a hand on Benjamin's arm. "How's Alexander? And Orua?"

"Alexander's doing better. He'll be released from the house of healing tomorrow."

"And Orua?"

He grimaced. "She's still alive."

It was like a spear had been driven into my gut. "Is she dying?"

"It doesn't look good."

I was so glad Maximus had been able to go to her. Feeling suddenly cold, I nodded and swam over to the wall opposite the window so that I wouldn't be seen by any guards in the corridor when Benjamin went through the privacy screen. The others followed my lead.

With a grimace, Benjamin swished through the screen to find Ti.

My heart pounded in my eardrums. We'd made it.

For now. I'd have to set aside my grief for Orua and my concern for Maximus until later. Too many lives depended on all of us keeping cool heads.

Depths, now I've netted in Benjamin as a co-conspirator.

I listened intently, straining to detect any sound out of the ordinary. A cough—Aunt Junia, I thought. The low murmuring of voices from near the front of the house. Then a shadow loomed in Benjamin's doorway.

"Well, well, well," said Ti quietly as she entered the room. "You certainly have a knack for getting into trouble."

"Senator Ti," said Carlina, reverence in her voice. "I've so wanted to meet you."

Ti scanned us all, something like amusement etched on

her features. "We can't have an open conversation here. Not with *them* out front."

"Well, we can't go anywhere else," I said. "We'll be found out. It was risky enough for the four of us to come here."

Ti's strong, curved nose twitched. "And I'm rather harder to hide, is what you're saying?"

"I didn't—"

She held up a hand. "No time to try to make yourself look better. It is what you meant, and it's not untrue."

Benjamin peeked through the curtain. "I'll distract them," he said. "Mother and I will go talk to them. Loudly. Until Ti comes to the front room and signals that it's safe."

"Urchin—"

But he was gone already.

"Athena!" he called from the far end of the corridor. "Any news of my sister?"

I winced. Now he really was a co-conspirator.

Now I heard Mother's voice, too. Benjamin must have tipped her off.

I motioned to Carlina, still trying to keep my voice quiet. "Senator, this is one of the leaders of the anti-monarchists, Carlina . . . " I glanced at Carlina in silent question.

"Rosopola," she said. "I'm Carlina Rosopola."

"Carlina, this is Senator Ti of Marbella."

"I suspect we both know who the other is," said Ti. "Your escapades in Elias's court have not gone unnoticed in the rest of the city."

"I didn't expect they had," I said. "Elias is quite angry, I expect."

She suppressed a chuckle. "He visited your mother here. I've never seen someone who pretends to be a leader act so much like a child."

I glanced at the others. "Of course, you've met Tor and Pippa before."

Ti dipped her head toward them. "Yes, of course."

"We came here because Carlina wanted to speak with you," I said. "And because we wanted your advice on the delicate situation we are all facing."

Ti's eyebrow curved upward. "By *delicate situation*, I suppose you mean the part where you publicly humiliated the crown prince and made yourselves fugitives?"

"Yes. That part."

"You, Jade, can likely throw yourself on Elias's mercy and get through the immediate crisis. Long-term, he will be dangerous for you. Pippa and Carlina, however, may not be so lucky."

"But I'm most to blame," I said.

"But Elias hopes Cleo will be useful to him. She was with the anti-monarchists for days. Even though they tried to keep her in the dark about their operations, she had occasion to observe their habits for an extended period of time. If he punishes her cherished daughter as a criminal, he will develop no goodwill with her. He will not get unfettered access to her information. And, by now, he may have acknowledged the dangers of alienating her, given the crown secrets she had access to under Stephanos. That doesn't mean he won't hold a grudge. But it means you're likely to be safe for now."

I chewed on a fingernail.

"In fact," said Ti, "he'll probably make a big show of pardoning you. Use it to highlight how *magnanimous* he is. He insinuated as much to your mother when he was here."

"It doesn't matter," I said. "Not if the others aren't safe. Especially Pippa."

Carlina squeaked in protest.

"You, too," I said, giving her an exasperated look, "but Pippa didn't ask to be brought into this."

Carlina chewed on her lip but nodded as if satisfied.

"This may be the time to be practical, Jade, not the time to float on principles." Ti studied me, and I looked down at the floor.

"She's right," said Pippa softly. "You're correct that I didn't ask to be in this position, but I made a choice, same as you. And I'm planning to move on soon, anyway. As soon as I can slip out unnoticed."

My head snapped up. "Elias is going to make a show of being magnanimous, you said?"

Ti's eyes narrowed, and her lips quirked to one side. "Yes, he suggested that."

"We can force his hand, then. You're right, it won't be for forever. But it will buy Carlina and me time, and give Pippa plenty of opportunity to make her exit safely, without fear of pursuit. And we won't even need to stage a coup."

"Stage a . . . coup?" Ti clutched a hand to her chest, looking more scandalized than I'd ever seen her. "I do not even want to know what you children came here to talk to me about."

"What's your plan, Jade?" Tor asked.

"We're going to box Elias into a corner. Let him go on and on about his benevolence and mercy and then force him to either pardon Pippa and Carlina or go back on his word about pardoning me."

Understanding dawned on Tor's face. "Because you won't accept the pardon unless he extends it to them."

"Exactly."

"Accept the pardon?" asked Ti. "I don't understand."

"It's an old custom," I said. "It's invoked as a formality whenever the king pardons someone. But it hasn't always been used as just a formality."

"No one's rejected a pardon in my lifetime," said Tor. "Maybe not even in my grandmother's lifetime."

"Which is exactly why it will draw so much attention. Elias can't punish me and save face after extending a pardon."

"This is an incredibly risky gambit," said Ti. "He could very well declare you ungrateful for his generosity and revoke it."

"But, as you said, Mother's cooperation is valuable to him."

"He will not be pleased that you're trying to outsmart him. Nor will he forget it."

"But it's more likely to buy us time than anything else I can think of. Would you rather we tried the coup? That *is* a line we could not uncross. But if he's willing to make this go away in exchange for Mother's cooperation, to dismiss my behavior as a youthful indiscretion driven by love of family, he could have the nobles eating out of the palm of his hand." The idea grew in my head, taking shape and unfurling into something that sounded crazy . . . but that just might work.

I'd have to watch my back as long as Elias stayed in power. Maybe for the rest of my life. But that was better than the alternatives.

Carlina floated forward. "But perhaps we should consider the idea of a coup—"

"Enough," said Ti. "Coups are for runaway governments that are so corrupt they cannot be reformed, salvaged, or redeemed. They are never to save the life of one person—or three people—particularly those who have put themselves in danger by breaking laws. The repercussions are devastating and far-reaching. Beyond what you can imagine. And even if the circumstances warranted it, with the Neptunian threat looming, it would be the pinnacle of foolishness. Unless they delay considerably in Marbella, power could not be consolidated in time to repel an invading army. I won't hear of this."

"I don't trust you to have confidence that my plan will work," I said, looking from Pippa to Carlina and back again. "I certainly don't expect—or even want—you to join me in the court when I do this. That way, if something goes wrong, I'm the only one at risk. And if Elias is that desperate for information out of Mother, I think the odds are in my favor."

Ti shook her head. "You don't lack impulsivity. I'll give

you that." She glanced back at the privacy screen. "I'll go before the guards get suspicious of your family. Be careful."

With a nod at each of us, she glided through the privacy curtain and out of sight. A few moments later, I heard her voice joining Mother's and Benjamin's at the end of the corridor.

Not long after, Benjamin reappeared in the doorway. "How'd it go?" he asked softly.

"As well as it could have, I think." I glanced at the others. "Carlina, Tor, Pippa, we'll go back to the safe place for tonight. Tomorrow, I'll go to Elias."

Benjamin choked.

"It will be okay, urchin. It's the best way to keep myself safe. Do me a favor?"

"Anything," he said.

"Find the friends and allies we still have. Get as many of them as you can in Elias's court at . . . high tide tomorrow morning. We'll make it a show."

CHAPTER

TWENTY-TWO

I didn't look fit to plead for my life when I glided into the king's court the next morning just after high tide. My hair billowed around my face when I moved, and my wrap was too simple for such a formal occasion. Part of me worried it was a fatal mistake when posturing for the status-conscious mer that milled about the back of the courtroom, blocking my view of the throne. But I was here now. Come what may.

I swam forward, my heart racing, and the mer began whispering among themselves, looking over at me. They were mostly friends of Mother's, but I nearly froze when I recognized Kora and Rhea in the crowd.

Rhea had come.

She'd betrayed me, tried to feed me to the sharks at Tor's trial, but she was here now. And that meant more than I could have imagined.

Kora offered me a little smile and a wave, but Rhea just floated there, looking down at the floor as though she wanted to sink into it. She and I had made peace, but surely she was still painfully aware of what she'd done. I was.

The crowd parted for me, and I caught the startled look on Elias's face when he saw me. Surely, he knew I was coming—there was a reason our allies were in the courtroom, after all—but based on his expression, I didn't think he'd really believed I'd show up.

Mother appeared from amid the congregated mer and swam alongside me as we approached Elias's chair below the throne.

I glanced up at the ornate throne beyond his chair, and realized, startled, that the coronation was tomorrow. Soon, Elias would be king.

"Let me talk first," Mother muttered in my ear.

"I think I've put my fin in my mouth enough times to last me a lifetime," I said.

When we reached our place about three tail-lengths from the crown prince, Mother said, "Your Majesty, I'm so pleased to see you in good health."

He eyed us with deep suspicion. "And I you, of course, Lady Cleo. Have you come to turn in your daughter for her treason?"

"I'd hoped you could see fit to overlook Lady Jade's offense, due to her young age and the tremendous pressure she's been under recently. You of all mer understand the pain that comes with sudden trauma. What Jade did was for my benefit. Surely, you cannot fault a child for wanting to save their parent? We are here to plead for your mercy."

I kept my eyes on the floor, trying to look every inch the submissive, repentant daughter.

Elias scoffed, and panic surged in my veins. He shifted in his chair. "Why should I extend forgiveness to someone who so flagrantly disobeyed my orders? Who assisted a mermaid guilty of fomenting open rebellion?"

Mother said, "Your Maj—"

"Because you're generous," I said, interrupting her. "And you desire to win the love of your subjects by a display of your magnanimity. I know it's not because I deserve it." Though my posture remained deferential, I met his eyes, a challenge dancing in mine.

He regarded me with barely veiled contempt. "You are correct. You do not deserve it." His mood seemed to lighten.

"Nevertheless, I believe in mercy and in celebration. My coronation is tomorrow, after all."

I forced my gills to remain steady, but calm flooded me at his words. The first part of the gambit had paid off. Something in his eyes warned me not to push my luck, but I couldn't escape my responsibility for my friends. I had gotten Pippa into this situation. I'd developed some sort of alliance with Carlina. The thought of abandoning them to the mercies of Elias made me sick to my stomach.

I schooled my features into a neutral expression. *Wait for the right moment.*

"Tell me, Lady Jade, why you and the naiad freed the revolutionary harpy."

I swallowed my anger. "I'd do anything to save my family, Your Majesty."

"Would you do it again?"

Yes. But it wouldn't do to say *that* aloud. "It's very hard to predict how one might behave in a moment of panic," I said instead. "All I could think about was what would happen if the revolutionaries killed my mother. We've lost so much. She's our stable reef in the midst of it all." This time there was no challenge in my eyes. I looked over at Mother. I meant every word.

He looked at me with an expression that almost seemed like hunger, and my stomach roiled. "Naive little starfish," he said.

I didn't react, but disgust filled me.

"Very well." He raised his hands toward the crowd. "I will extend a pardon to Lady Jade as a show of my love for my citizens and my gracious nature."

I knew Elias would posture, but his moods changed so frequently it made me afraid. I'd been concerned that he was weak, that he could be manipulated by his advisors, but might this suggest a different kind of instability. What if Carlina was right? What if we needed Theo on the throne instead?

No time to worry about that right now.

I dipped my head. "Thank you, Your Majesty. It is a great relief to hear that you are so merciful." *Draw him out. Make it so he cannot withdraw the pardon without losing face.*

"But of course," he said. "A king lives for the best interests of his people. It is my great delight to pardon an offense."

I caught a glimpse of Theo emerging from one of the small council rooms along the far wall—though not the one Pippa, Carlina, and I had escaped from. That one was covered in thick netting to conceal the hole the soldiers had broken open in the door. Theo and I made eye contact for the barest of moments.

I had to draw Elias out more. Perhaps even make him think it was his idea.

"You are more gracious even than your late father," I blurted.

Mother elbowed me sharply.

Elias's eyes narrowed as if trying to detect the reason for my flattery, but then he looked out at the crowd. After a moment, he relaxed. "Well, Lady Jade, there was no better man to teach me how to be king than my father. I seek always to live up to his legacy and even exceed it."

"I think you will." I met his gaze and held it, ignoring the chill that had taken hold of me. "His Majesty, King Stephanos, of course, sheltered the Wye and Camford naiads in Thessalonike for several years before the unfortunate incident with the Guard. I'm sure you would like to celebrate the best parts of his legacy."

"Ah." He inclined his head toward me. "You are concerned for the fate of the naiad who assisted you in your . . . indiscretion."

With a half-shrug, I dropped my gaze. "Of course, Your Majesty."

"She, too, shall be pardoned. I declare it."

Equal parts thrill and relief ran through me, but I also

felt a thread of concern that he was so easily manipulated. Surely—

The doors to the court burst open, and a captain of the Guard swam in at top speed. "Urgent message for His Majesty," he said, his gills pulsing rapidly.

"Depths, Caiaphas," said Elias, studying him. "What is it?"

Caiaphas stopped alongside me and straightened. "A scout just brought word from the outer reef. The Neptunians are encamped a mere five leagues from the city."

CHAPTER

TWENTY-THREE

"I see," said Elias. He suddenly looked even smaller in his chair. How would he look when he'd officially taken the throne, I wondered? Would he still seem like he couldn't quite fill his father's seat? Or would he find some new strength within himself? "How many enemy soldiers are we talking about?"

"The scout could not see the end of their encampment without risking discovery. At least a thousand. Possibly double that."

I blanched. So did Elias.

Elias closed his eyes and gripped the edge of his hammock chair. "Call up every member of the Guard."

Theo swam toward Elias, his movements confident and sure. "And every able-bodied mer in the city. Arm them. Give them blades, even."

Elias's eyes flew open. "Any mer who strikes down a Neptunian will be pardoned of any offense they have committed in the past. And send word to the queen of White Cove. Have her ready her ships to come to our aid."

Overlander allies, I realized in relief. *Must have been through Felix's trade contacts.* Perhaps the skub had earned his pardon after all.

Even though I'd seen the invaders with my own eyes in Marbella, the thought of an invasion was surreal. The beat of my heart seemed to drum an ominous refrain: *Nothing will ever be the same. Nothing will ever be the same.*

Even if we won—which seemed, at best, doubtful—this battle would leave a scar on the city for a generation. How many would die?

How many mer I loved would die?

"You are dismissed," Elias said to Mother and me, looking past us, as if part of him had already forgotten that we were there.

I nodded. I hadn't extracted a promise of Carlina's pardon, but Elias had bigger problems to worry about than a stray anti-monarchist. For now, at least, she was safe.

And with the Neptunians almost at our gates, *now* might be all we had.

The advisors congregated around the crown prince, leaning in to discuss the situation at hand. I caught a few snatches of what they were saying, something about *overlanders*, and *numbers*, and *contingency plans*. I glanced from them to Mother, wondering whether she would join them. But she shook her head and turned to leave the court. She was no longer one of them. With a profound feeling of loss and fear, I followed in her wake.

⌒

"Jade!" Alexander bolted up out of his bed when I appeared in his doorway at the house of healing, Mother lingering behind me. "What are you doing here? I heard—"

"I'm fine," I said, darting to his side and pushing him back down into the hammock. I gave him a soft kiss on the cheek. "Elias doesn't care about that right now."

He blinked several times at me. "What happened? Why doesn't he care?"

"He was posturing," I said. "In the middle of extending a pardon to me when word came that the Neptunians are close."

"Already?" His face paled, and he gripped my hands more tightly.

"Yes." I nodded. "Much sooner than I'd hoped."

"We can assume that they took Marbella, then. Easily."

"We already knew that," I murmured.

"It seemed likely. And Marbella is a larger city."

Mother's hand brushed my shoulder. "We need to go, Jade. The physicians have said Alexander can leave, especially in light of . . . everything. We'll take him home with us."

"We need to get Pippa, too."

Mother nodded. "Of course. But let's get Alexander home first. He still has some recovering to do."

"No time for recovery if the Neptunians are here," Alexander said. "We all need to fight."

I chewed on my lower lip, but I had no argument. We'd all fight together, or we'd all be conquered together.

Or, more likely, both. Delightful.

"Well," said Mother, "the Neptunians aren't in the city yet. You'll recover as long as you can before they arrive, and I won't hear of any disagreement. You took a hard blow to the head. How are you feeling now?"

"Still a little confused, sometimes." His hand drifted up toward his light-brown hair, near his injury. "But the headache is gone."

She cast a serious glance at him, but my heart felt warm in my chest. Mother had always kept Alexander at arm's length. And here she was, worrying about him. Even amid all the fear and doubt whirling around us, I couldn't suppress the small smile that came to my lips. She'd said before she left that she thought we'd be a good match. I'd chalked it up to the stress of the situation garbling her mind. But maybe he was winning her over after all.

Or maybe we were all just terrified.

As if she could read my thoughts, she shot me a glare and then turned back to Alexander. "Come. Gather your things if you have any."

Alexander held out empty hands. "Nope. Not with me."

She nodded. "We'll go tell the physician out front that you're leaving, and we'll get you settled back at Junia's."

"Can we go home?" I asked. "To our house? There's more room for everyone, and I miss it."

"Most of the new furniture isn't in yet," she said, studying me. "It may not feel like home."

"I don't care," I said. "We'll make do."

"Well, there's no harm in it, I suppose." She glanced up at the ceiling and then nodded. "Yes. It will be good to be home. And easier to fit everyone we've seemed to gather around us. We can bring over a couple more hammocks from Junia's."

"And I don't mind sleeping on the floor. As long as there's a cloak to rest on."

Alexander winced and touched his head. "I think I might mind sleeping on the floor."

I chuckled. "That's not an option for you. Injuries earn you a hammock bed. So does being old." I shot a wink at Mother.

She ignored me. "Do you need any help swimming, Alexander?"

He floated upward and then toward us slowly, as if testing each muscle. "I don't believe so. But thank you. I'll say something if I need help."

"See that you do." She turned abruptly and swam out the door and down the corridor.

I reached out and took Alexander's hand. He held my gaze with a look of love and adoration that soothed the deepest part of me. Yes, I knew I wanted to spend the rest of my life with this merman. No matter how long or short the rest of my life turned out to be. "Together?"

"Always."

TWENTY-FOUR

The next two days melded together in a blur of activity. The crier announced the delay of the coronation and Elias's amnesty to everyone who took up arms against the invaders, and mer once again seemed to disappear from the canals, staying indoors for everything but the most essential errands. I still traveled to the house of healing once a day to check on Orua's prognosis. Maximus was at her bedside always, day and night. She was stable, the physicians said, but they wouldn't say whether or not they thought she'd survive.

I kept hoping.

But even though we kept ourselves busy—getting everyone, including Aunt Junia, settled into my house, preparing a cache of weapons, securing and re-securing the windows—it all somehow felt pointless. Like we were occupying the time to distract ourselves from the sense of impending doom.

We have advance warning, I kept reminding myself. *And the Neptunians don't know that. They expect to catch us as unaware as they caught Marbella.*

Unless Octavian had defected and told them that a group of Thessalonikens had escaped.

Alexander and I were sitting at a brand-new table in the kitchen when a knock sounded at the door.

"I'll get it!" called Mother. Now that every member of the Guard had been called to the wall, we were on our own against anyone who might try to do us harm. But I suspected we were no longer high on anyone's priority list. Even the anti-monarchists had better things to do than harass us.

Like a plan for how to stay alive.

All of Thessalonike was on alert, instructed to do whatever they could to repel the intruders when they came. Most of the city seemed to be preparing for the fight of their lives. Though some murmurings from mer in the canal told us that others were skeptical that it was in our best interests to fight. If we were woefully outmatched, better to surrender quietly to minimize the loss of life and prevent the destruction of the city.

I didn't know who was right.

"Oh. Hello, girls," Mother said from the door. "Can I help you?"

A quiet, feminine voice answered. I couldn't quite make out the words, but I recognized the voice.

Kora. I clenched Alexander's hand where we sat at the table.

"That will be up to Jade," Mother said. "Wait here."

I heard the gentle sound of the door closing and looked up at Alexander. "What do I do?" I whispered.

"Do you want to see her?" he asked.

"I-I don't know. Everything was so—"

Mother poked her head into the room. "If you didn't hear, Kora and Rhea are at the door. They want to talk to you."

Kora *and* Rhea. My hands felt weak.

But if we might all die in the next week, I should probably see my friends—*former* friends—now. We might not have many more opportunities.

"You can let them in," I said, my voice stronger than I felt. "Send them back here. I'd like Alexander in the room when I talk to them."

"Are you sure?" Mother asked. "You don't look particularly happy about it."

"I'm sure."

With a shrug, she swam back down the corridor toward the front door. A moment later, I heard her voice. "Jade is back in the kitchen. You can go talk to her."

"Thank you," said Kora.

I tried to relax as I counted the moments.

Then Kora and Rhea swam into the room, and my heart flopped painfully in my chest.

"Hey," I said. What else was there to say?

"Hey, Jade," said Kora. "It's good to see you, Alexander."

Rhea remained silent, her gaze fixed on the far wall.

"I-we came to see how you are," said Kora. "And apologize. We both have a lot to apologize for, actually."

"Me more than Kora," Rhea blurted. "Jade, I really am sorry. I know we made peace right after the massacre, but it's still just eating me up inside, and I don't know what to do except beg for your forgiveness." She made eye contact with me, her chin trembling. "It's worse with everything going on in the city right now—what if I die, or you do, and we've just left things like this?"

Kora set a hand gently on Rhea's arm. "And I've ignored you since . . . everything started. I let a wedge be driven between us because I was afraid of other mer. I let concern for my own status be more important than loyalty." Her voice quavered. "That was rotten of me. I knew it at the time. There's no excuse."

The layers of resentment in my heart gradually gave way to something else. Love, perhaps? I'd been willing to work with Tor, even after all he'd done. Why couldn't I rekindle a friendship with Kora and Rhea?

"I . . . " My voice cracked. "We were friends our whole lives. Since our very first year in school. It was really . . . hard, with all that history between us, to watch things unfold the way they did. I wish we could raise that sunken ship from the depths, but . . . "

I couldn't continue. The emotions were too overwhelming. Too intense.

"I'm sorry," Kora said. "It's okay if you can't. Really. I just—"

"No." I shook my head. "I didn't let you in to send you away like this. Just . . . give me a moment." My gills heaved.

They both nodded.

I closed my eyes and tried to suppress the violent torrent of emotions that stirred in my chest. Forgiveness was hard. Especially when my friends hadn't been there for me at my lowest point. When one of them had betrayed me, lying in front of the whole city to take Tor's side against mine in the trial.

How could I let that go?

But how could I not? After so many years with them at my side. In the face of impending destruction. How could I risk never getting the chance to reconcile with them?

I opened my eyes. There was something about Rhea that seemed . . . older, somehow. More serious. As though she'd aged five years in the last three months. "If we all make it through this," I said, "there will be a lot of cleaning up to do in our friendship. We can't just pretend none of this happened. I don't know that things can ever go all the way back to what they were before. But I do want to try to mend things if we can. I want that very much."

"Oh, Jade. Really? That's all we ask," said Kora. "I . . . " She trailed off.

They floated there awkwardly for a few moments, and then Kora said, "We'll go. But thanks, Jade. You didn't have to say that."

"Yes," I said, drifting upward, "I did. Because it's true." I swam to them and gave them each a brief hug. "We'll figure this out, somehow."

I swam with them to the door and watched as they swam down the canal toward their own homes. Then, with a little flare of my gills, I returned to the table to sit with Alexander.

"Neptunian skubs," I muttered. "Can't they just get here already so we know the outcome one way or another?"

Alexander chuckled darkly. "Let's enjoy the days we have, love."

Pippa came into the room with a serious expression on her face. "Hey," she said. Every day she reiterated her plans to strike out for the coast, but every day she'd delayed.

"You're going to run out of time," I said.

"I know."

Concern flared in my chest. "So you've decided to stay?"

"I wanted to wait until Lady Cleo was back so I knew you all were safe. If I leave before the Neptunians come, I'll live the rest of my life not knowing what happened to any of you. That's why I'm putting it off." Pippa shrugged. "But those were your friends? The ones who . . . "

"There's no way to phrase that charitably," I said. "Yes, that was Kora and Rhea."

"I couldn't help but overhear," she said. "I'm proud of you."

"You're a lot better at this than I am. You extended grace to Tor, after everything he did to your family and your community. Kora and Rhea are perfection itself in comparison to him."

"There's a lot we have to forgive, or we'll never be able to move on to better things."

"How did you get so wise?"

"Well," she said with a little smile. "Anna was pretty wise for her years. So was my older brother—the one who died shortly after we left the rivers. And my parents. I guess I'm just trying to live in a way that would make all of them proud."

I could relate to that.

"Anyway," she said. "I liked your response to them. I'm

going to go lie down for a while. Who knows how many more opportunities for a nap I'll have before the fighting begins." She said it as if it were a joke.

"Very funny," I said, my lips quirked.

"You have to be able to laugh!" she called as she walked away from the kitchen and toward the vertical corridor that led up to the sleeping chambers.

"You have to be able to laugh," I murmured.

Alexander reached out and caressed my cheek. "We find joy where we can."

I leaned over and kissed him back, trying to let the peace of the moment wash away the grief of the past and the fear of the future. For who knew how many more moments of peace we had left.

CHAPTER

TWENTY-FIVE

The next day, rumors began to spread through the city that the Neptunians had been sighted a mere league away. If they had drawn so near, the attack was imminent. In the front room of the house, I sat on the floor with my back up against the wall, and ran my hand over the kitchen blade we'd repurposed into an offensive weapon for me to wield. The handle was short, and the edge not as sharp as I'd like, but it was better than nothing.

Every noise in the canal sent my heart into my throat. But the Neptunians hadn't arrived yet.

A knock sounded on the door, and I moved upward and to the right to answer it.

Tor waited on the other side.

"Oh. Hello," I said, drawing back, on my guard. "What are you doing here?"

He held something out to me, handle-first. A blade. Realization flooded me. This was not just any blade. It belonged to me. A gift from my mother, that Tor had stolen from me the night he'd almost killed me.

I dropped the kitchen knife, reached out slowly, and took my blade from him. The weight felt right in my hands.

"At first, I kept it because I wanted to turn it in to the inspectors and have you arrested for drawing a blade on me," he said. "And then, once I realized . . . well, everything, I kept it because I couldn't imagine the conversation we'd have when I brought it back. But it's a good weapon. You should have it today."

Clutching the blade, I stared at him with a questioning expression.

He waved his hand. "I don't want to talk about it. Not really. I just . . . we're all thinking about what we need to make right. That was one thing I *could* still make right." He floated backward. "Goodbye. Safe currents."

"You, too," I said. What else was there to say?

He turned around and swam down the canal. Confusion hovered around me. Then, with a little laugh, I shook my head. Mer were complicated. Even someone like Tor was capable of good as well as evil. I didn't know at what point the good outweighed or covered over the bad, or if it ever could. But I was happy to have my blade back.

I inspected it. It was still in pristine condition. Tor had even sharpened it for me. Though it was primarily a decorative piece, the handle was sturdy and the blade deadly. I hated the idea of using it in a battle.

I clenched the handle. But I would use it. Tor was right. It was a good blade. Better than the knife I'd been planning to use.

When it came down to it, I didn't know whether I could actually wield a blade in violence. It ran contrary to our time-honored traditions, to everything we held dear. Except in times of dire communal need, we did not spill blood in the water, lest we bring sharks—or webbed-foot dragons—down on the city.

There had never been an exception to that rule in my lifetime—nor in my mother's or grandmother's generations.

But here we were facing an invasion, instructed to use blades against the enemy. Perhaps the inevitable sharks would kill more Neptunians than we would.

I closed the door and turned to swim up to my chamber. With any luck, I'd get a little time alone, in silence, before the Neptunians came.

It was not to be.

No sooner had I sunk down on my hammock than I heard a shout in the distance. I tensed, listening. Was this it? Had they come?

Then another shout.

A scream.

They're here.

"Jade! Benjamin! Pippa!" Mother yelled from the first level of the house.

Benjamin and I emerged from our chambers into the corridor, each clutching our blades. His knife had also been a gift from Mother, sturdily wrought, with a black handle that curved upward on each side into sharp points that paralleled the blade.

"Stay here and try to hide," I said as we swam down the vertical corridor to find Mother.

"No." Benjamin shook his head. "The whole city is fighting. So will I."

"Urchin, you're still a child."

"I'm only three years younger than you."

We spilled out into the front room to find Mother, Aunt Junia, and Alexander waiting.

"Everyone will fight," said Mother, her face grim. "Even my own children. But we will not seek out the battle. We will defend our own canal. We will wait for it to come to us. In the meantime, beg the tides that the Guard will be able to keep most of the attackers at bay and that we will not be dealing with a whole battalion on our own."

"Should have sent the Guard to Marbella's aid when we had the chance. Taken the Neptunians by surprise," I muttered.

"There are many things Elias should have done differently," Mother said. "That is one of them."

Ti emerged from the second level with a bludgeon in her hand. "I'm ready to do my part against the dayedae who conquered my city."

I wasn't sure what *dayedae* meant exactly, but the cold expression on her face made her intent perfectly clear.

"For home," said Mother.

"For home," we intoned after her.

Mother kissed Benjamin on the forehead and then pulled me into a swift embrace. "I'll go first," she said.

Aunt Junia fumbled with her blade and nearly dropped it.

"Aunt Junia!" I called, rushing to her side. "Are you not feeling well? Should you be resting?"

She shot me a wry look. "I'm not dying, child."

"You can't fight. Not with the enervia."

Something like sadness shone in her eyes. "I won't leave everyone else to the spears of the Neptunians. Besides, if you all die, and only I am captured, I'm as good as dead in my condition. We fight as one."

I'd seen that expression before, usually on Mother's face. The raw determination. The stubbornness that defied anyone to tell her differently. There would be no dissuading Aunt Junia from joining us in the canal.

"Alright," Mother said, her voice almost shaking. "Let's go."

I followed Mother out the door and into the darkening water. It was a cloudy day above the surface, leaving the ocean a murky gray.

I swallowed.

The commotion was coming from the eastern side of the city, far from us. But the Neptunians could swim over the walls anywhere. Perhaps the first attack was only a diversion. Hadn't we seen them swarm into Marbella with an unstoppable force?

A contingent of the Guard swam down our canal, sweeping their gaze back and forth as if looking for any stray Neptunians who had entered the city.

Maximus was among them. I nodded at him and saw raw pain and anger raging in his eyes.

"Maximus!" I called, unable to stop myself.

He nodded at the others to continue and stopped, turning toward me. "Is something wrong?" he asked.

"No." I shook my head. "I just wanted to wish you safe tides. And to thank you for all you've done."

"Orua's dead," he said.

A bitter taste rose up in my mouth, and my stomach sank as though it were weighted down with stones.

"I'm so sorry," I said.

"Me too." He drove a hand through his hair in a short, jerky motion. "I can't believe she's gone. But I can't think about it. I can't. I have a job to do. A city to defend. I'll mourn her later if I'm so unfortunate as to survive this battle."

I thought he was jesting at first, but the agony in his eyes suggested no laugh. His family was nearly gone. His beloved was dead. All he had left was his mother, and I didn't know what their relationship was like.

"I'm sorry, Jade," he said. "I appreciate your words. Go in peace."

"Peace be upon you."

He turned and swam away with rough, uneven thrashes of his fin. I bit the inside of my cheek. How many more would die before this was over?

Too many.

I reached back and ruffled Benjamin's hair, just in case I wouldn't get a chance to do it again.

"Hey." He swiped at my hand. "Don't forget I'm armed!"

I snorted, but it felt forced. I couldn't get Orua's face out of my mind. My gills flared, and I scanned in every direction for a sign of incoming Neptunians. "I could take you in a fight any day, urchin."

"Could not."

"Keep your voices down, children," Mother cautioned. "We don't want to draw attention to ourselves."

There were other groups coming out of houses now,

huddling in doorways, waiting. Those who had decided to fight for the city. Others were no doubt hiding in their homes, waiting for resolution to the conflict one way or another.

Maximus was right. We couldn't mourn the dead. Not now.

Three Neptunians streaked through the water above us, so high up they were nearly at the surface. They each rode a hippocampus, and even though fear pulsed in every part of my body, I couldn't help but admire the majestic creatures that boasted a tail like a mer but a front half like a . . . what had Pippa called that overland creature again? A horse?

"Stay where you are," murmured Mother. "We wait until they come to our canal."

Five members of the Guard shot upward from a nearby canal, giving chase to the Neptunians. I squinted but couldn't tell if it was Maximus's group. One of the Neptunians shrieked when a Thessaloniken soldier stabbed him through with a spear. Blood flowed from the wound and plumed in the water around the Neptunian.

I froze, staring at the blood that formed a sickening cloud floating up toward the surface and down toward the seafloor. *Blood in the water.*

The Neptunian slumped over across the neck of his hippocampus, and his companions shrieked and turned on the Guard with brutal force. One cleaved a mermaid in half with his long sword, and the other plunged his trident all the way through a merman.

The water above us was turning crimson now, and I thought I might vomit.

Another hippocampus—this one riderless—soared above us and toward the city wall. Had his rider been killed? Captured?

And then a mermaid—no older than Benjamin—screamed

from four houses down. As one, we whirled toward her and saw a burly Neptunian at reef level, staring down at us from the end of the canal.

TWENTY-SIX

Deadly calm overtook me as I studied the Neptunian. I panicked about the most inane things on a daily basis, but with death staring me in the face, fear couldn't touch me. I gripped my blade.

Let him come.

He was taller than most of the mer of Thessalonike, with broad shoulders and jet-black hair that fell in a long braid down his chest. His armor was as black as his hair and covered in decorative silver spikes, and he wielded a dark, barbed trident. His hippocampus, too, boasted armor—thin plates of slate-gray metal that also boasted silver spikes.

Mother raised her blade—a decorative sword she'd bought for her own chamber—and began moving toward the Neptunian. I followed at her side, a hand-length behind. Alexander pressed close at my side.

"Don't engage first," I said to him. "Please. Not with your injury."

"I'm fine, Jade," he said, but I reached out and pushed him an arm's length backward. He grumbled but didn't move up to float even with me.

We passed the teenage mermaid and her parents and continued moving forward until we were three or four tail-lengths from the Neptunian.

"Get out," Mother said, authority resounding in her voice.

The Neptunian laughed, a quieter laugh than I'd expected, in a tenor voice. With his fierce appearance, I'd expected it to be deeper. "I don't take orders from you." His accent was thick, but the words were recognizable enough.

"Who do you take orders from?" Mother asked.

The question surprised me.

It seemed to surprise the Neptunian as well. He raised an eyebrow. "From my captain. Or the general."

"And what is the name of this general?" asked Mother.

"She is Salacia Amphitrite of Tethys, daughter of the ocean."

I tried not to roll my eyes.

He straightened astride his hippocampus. "And all this bloodshed will stop the moment your king bows to her."

"We have no king," I said.

He scoffed. "Of course you do. Romulus Tertinius brought us the news of your city."

"A lot has happened since your spy left," said Mother. "The king is dead. You're dealing with an unseasoned princeling with no judgment and no sense of duty. What kind of losses will your army take when every last mer in this city fights to the death?"

He glanced over at the family cowering behind us. "I am terribly afraid of the mer of this city."

Without even a change in facial expression, he dismounted his hippocampus and advanced on Mother, his sword at the ready. Mother swam at him, but he shunted her blade aside with his trident and twisted his wrist, jerking her sword free of her hands. As it floated to the ground, he drew his weapon back to strike Mother. With a yell, I darted toward her, but before I could reach them, he froze, his trident not even halfway toward Mother.

In the confusion, Mother recovered her blade and turned to face him. Blood curled upward from eight small holes in his body, and his eyes were glazed like he was already dead.

"What . . . " Realization dawned on me, and I turned to look at Pippa, who had taken up a position behind me and to the left. Her hands were extended and her fingers pointed at the Neptunian.

"Water-spears," I whispered.

She shrugged. "Good thing I didn't leave." Her face was hard, but she looked haunted, as if she couldn't quite believe what she'd done.

The hippocampus moved toward his rider and let out a plaintive sound, like a rolling bell. He nudged the body of the Neptunian with his nose. Was he trying to wake him up?

Pippa took a sharp step backward.

I whirled toward her and reached out a hand to steady her. "Pippa. Are you okay?"

She shook her head five or six times, as if trying to shake the memory out. "I've never killed someone," she murmured.

"I know, I know." I pulled her trembling body into a hug.

"Alexander, come with me," Mother said. "Help me drag the body two canals over, to the shops. That canal should be abandoned. No sense leaving it here to catch the attention of the other Neptunians. Jade, Pippa, keep an eye on everyone."

"We will," said Pippa. She stepped backward out of my hug, clenching her fists at her side. "I will be fine. It was him or Cleo. It had to be done."

Mother and Alexander each took a shoulder of the Neptunian and dragged him around the hippocampus and toward the end of the canal. The hippocampus followed, letting out a shrill cry like what I'd always imagined a wraith sounded like. I shivered.

"Should we help it?" Benjamin asked, looking at the creature.

"I think it's mourning," I said. Mother and Alexander disappeared around the corner, the hippocampus at their side.

"Behind us!" called Ti.

I turned, still feeling calm and collected. This time, three Neptunians rode their steeds on the canal that intersected with ours. I clutched my blade and darted to the front of the group to shield Benjamin and Aunt Junia, but the Neptunians merely smirked and continued on their way down the other canal. Looking for the Guard, perhaps?

I thanked the tides they were moving in the opposite direction of Mother and Alexander.

Yells sounded from somewhere behind us, several canals away. The Neptunians were infiltrating our entire neighborhood. A lot of them.

With a determined clench of my jaw, I turned back around, facing the direction in which Mother and Alexander had disappeared—no, from which they would return. *Come on. Stay safe. One, two, three . . .*

By the time I'd counted to one hundred, they were still nowhere to be seen. The fear flooded over me, spreading outward from my chest to each fingertip. Surely, any moment Mother and Alexander would round the corner and come back into view. I started counting again.

One. Two. Three.

Again, I reached one hundred, and my heartbeat spiked. But I couldn't go find them. They could take care of themselves in a way that Aunt Junia couldn't. I glanced over at Pippa. She was the most powerful of us all. By a long shot. Could I leave her with the others and try to find Mother and Alexander? But every time we split up, we took a risk.

They'd be back soon.

I started counting again.

I had just reached *fifty-six* when Mother and Alexander rounded the corner, a reddish tint on both of their blades.

"Alexander! Mother!" I flew toward them, bowling Alexander over with a hug. "You're okay? What happened?"

"We encountered an invader," Mother said. "She nearly did us in, but the two of us fighting in tandem managed a lucky strike. We . . . have no chance against these trained soldiers." She gazed down the canal in both directions. "Perhaps the Guard will fare better, but being in the canals is a death sentence for the rest of us."

I looked back toward the surface. The ships that were supposed to come to our aid still weren't here, but a single hammerhead shark was silhouetted against the sunlight.

Depths. The sharks were here already. Dragons wouldn't be far behind.

Where are the ships?

If our allies didn't come, was there any way to save the city?

Defend the canal. One skirmish at a time.

A contingent of the Royal Mer Guard spilled into our canal. I searched for anyone I knew among them and found Maximus at the outskirts of the battalion and Tor at his side. I tried to catch their eyes, but they were both staring back the way they'd come. In fact, so were the other soldiers. Something uncomfortable tingled in my stomach.

They're coming.

I looked up again at the surface, which was tinged with a sheen of blood. No sign of the hammerhead shark anymore, or of the ships that were supposed to be here, for that matter.

Biting my lip, I followed the gaze of the Guard, waiting for something to happen.

When the first Neptunian came around the corner, my gills flared. She was tall and elegant, wearing silver-spiked black armor and riding a white hippocampus. She gripped a trident in her long, slender fingers. Two more Neptunians followed her, and then five more.

After that, I stopped counting.

A sea of Neptunians congregated at the end of our canal. They outnumbered the contingent of the Guard at least three to one. And they were coming for us.

"Surrender!" called the mermaid leading them. "We desire no more bloodshed."

I whispered to Pippa. "Any chance you can take all of them out?"

She cracked her knuckles. "Some of them. But this is a losing battle. This whole thing is."

"Just get through this skirmish," said Mother. "We'll worry about the rest later."

I almost laughed at the absurdity of her statement. *Skirmish?* This was about to be a bloodbath. Even if Pippa had found the strength to wield the ocean itself with considerable power, even with twenty soldiers on our side, we were staring death in the face.

"Perhaps we should go inside and wait it out," I said. "We may be spared if we're willing to submit to their leadership."

"No," said Pippa, flexing her fingers. "I'm done *submitting* to tyrants."

The Neptunians advanced toward the Guard. "If no one will speak a word of surrender," called the leader, "we will have to destroy you."

A hammerhead—I wasn't sure if it was the same one I'd seen earlier—swam directly over our roof and toward the gathered crowd. I suppressed a shriek.

Not good, not good, not good.

A few members of the Guard had noticed it, too, casting it sidelong glances before looking back at the Neptunians.

The elegant mermaid raised her trident. "Your blood is in your own waters," she cried.

Then the Neptunians charged.

CHAPTER
TWENTY–SEVEN

The Neptunians slammed into the Guard, shrieking an eerie battle cry that made my arms go cold. I couldn't register anything specific that was happening in the melee, but from what I could see, the Neptunians were striking down the Guard with ruthless efficiency. A red mist of blood swirled all around us.

Pippa charged to the front of our ground and shaped water spear after water spear, hurling them at the Neptunians that broke through the line of the Guard.

An intrusive, irrelevant thought kept circling in my head: what an idiot King Stephanos had been to level an attack on the naiads. Pippa had been right when she'd said that if they'd chosen to fight back they could have taken the whole city.

And if they hadn't left us behind, with the naiads at our side and notice of the Neptunians arrival, we'd have stood a chance.

Survive this skirmish. I could hear Mother's voice in my head.

The hammerhead burst into the cloud of blood and tore apart a shrieking Neptunian before fading back into the red water.

A Neptunian came at us from the right, and I whirled to face him and then fell backward, sinking to the seafloor at the sight of his long, vicious trident. I couldn't move. Even my gills felt frozen, useless. My blade could do nothing against his weapon. I was about to die.

He advanced on me, and then Alexander lurched into him from the side, stabbing him in the kidney with a kitchen blade.

The Neptunian shook Alexander off with a roar and turned on him, but his movements were stilted and shaky. Subpar weapon or not, Alexander had struck a significant blow.

Move.

I gathered myself and flew at the Neptunian, my weapon drawn, but Alexander had gripped the handle of the trident and wrested it from his grasp.

Alexander leveled the weapon at the Neptunian. "Leave," he hissed.

Blood curled upward from the wound in the Neptunian's side, diffusing into the red-tinged seawater that was starting to choke my gills. He lurched toward Alexander, swiping at the trident to try to take it back. With something like compassion in his eyes, Alexander plunged the trident into the Neptunian's torso and ripped it back out again.

The Neptunian blinked, sinking to the seafloor, the lifeblood draining from him.

I whirled back to take stock of the situation just in time to see a Neptunian raise her trident at me. I dropped my blade and grasped at the trident's handle instead, trying to wrest it from her like Alexander had done. To my right, I saw another Neptunian coming at me. There were too many. I jerked harder at the trident.

The second Neptunian drew a sword, and I braced myself for searing pain. But it didn't come. Still gripping the trident handle, I turned my head to see that Aunt Junia had thrown herself in front of the Neptunian's sword, and it had sliced into her chest.

"No!" I screamed. Rage overcame me, and in one sharp

move, I wrested the trident from the mermaid who had attacked me and speared her with it. Then I turned and drove the trident into the chest of the merman who had wounded Aunt Junia before he could remove his sword from her body. I shoved him away, the trident still sticking out of him.

Then I sank to the seafloor with Aunt Junia and grasped her right hand.

She was still alive.

The battle was raging all around me now, but I didn't care. I didn't care about anything except making sure Aunt Junia didn't die alone.

She smiled. "Jade."

"I'm here." I leaned over her and clutched her hand more tightly. Her other hand came up to caress my face.

"My child," she whispered.

She stared up at the surface, her eyes losing focus, and I knew the tides had taken her. With one final squeeze of her hand, I forced my attention back to the battle at hand.

Aunt Junia had died for me. It should have been me dying on the seafloor. And I would make sure I didn't squander the gift she'd given me. I darted to the Neptunian merman I'd killed and yanked the trident from his body before floating upward to study the battle.

Something had changed.

The Neptunians seemed fewer and further between. Then it struck me. *Reinforcements.* More of the Guard had come to our aid.

Mother and Ti were fending off an attacking soldier, and I swam to them to help drive him off, but already the battle was growing thinner. The Neptunian spun away and swam off to seek an easier fight. I whirled around again, looking for more danger, but the Neptunians had retreated to fight in another canal. I slumped over.

"Junia!" Mother yelled, her eyes landing on her sister's body. She dropped her blade and bolted to Junia's side. "Don't leave me," she said, her voice as distraught as I'd ever heard it. "Please stay."

But I knew Aunt Junia was already gone. My chin quivered. Aunt Junia was gone, and I was still here. I flicked my fin to swim to Mother, laying one hand on her shoulder. Bending down, I used my other hand to close Aunt Junia's eyes.

"It was for me," I said.

"What?" Mother asked, her voice catching.

"I was being attacked by two Neptunians at once. Aunt Junia blocked a blow intended for me."

Mother wrapped me in her arms, her body shaking. At first, she said nothing, and then she managed, "She loved you like you were her own. She always did."

"I know." The sobs overcame me then, wracking my whole body. "I—" My voice cracked, and I couldn't say anything else.

Why had we fought? What was the point? The city would fall anyway, and we'd have to adjust to life under Neptunian rule, whatever that looked like. And now we'd have to do it without the stable, supporting force of Aunt Junia in our lives. It felt like a Neptunian trident had slashed through my stomach.

Father. George. Aunt Junia. My family was almost gone. I sat up. "Benjamin. Is Benjamin alright?"

"I'm here," said Benjamin from behind me, his voice tired but strong.

"I'm here too." Alexander set a hand on my shoulder.

Pippa knelt on the other side of Aunt Junia's body, her gaze vacant.

So, we'd all survived. All except Aunt Junia.

My gills flared. The water was choking, toxic, filled with the blood of the dead. And who knew where the sharks were—metaphorical and otherwise.

"Let's get her inside," I said. "Staunch the wound. Prepare her for a proper burial."

"We'll get out of the blood, anyway," said Ti. "Regroup."

Alexander offered to help, but I shrugged him off, and Mother and I carried Aunt Junia toward our door. With a nod, Alexander swam ahead of us to open it.

"Grab some chilyo paste," I said to him. "Meet us in Mother's chamber."

We carried Aunt Junia up the corridor to the second level of the house and down the hallway to Mother's room. We laid Aunt Junia's body in Mother's sleeping hammock, and a shudder wracked my core.

"She would have thought it a worthy death," said Mother, her voice steady again. "She'd have been proud."

Alexander appeared in the doorway with the chilyo paste, and Mother reached for it and began coating Aunt Junia's wound. I swam to the window and opened it to see if I could get a sense of how the battle for the city was going. Far to the left, I could see signs of another skirmish, but the sheen of red lay too thick over the city for me to get a good view of anything. I moved to close the window to keep the blood out of the house, but stopped short at the shadows I saw on the surface.

The overlander ships had arrived.

TWENTY-EIGHT

Only after I'd closed and secured the window did I realize that I hadn't checked to see if Maximus had survived the onslaught. But it could wait. We had grief enough to reckon with for now.

But what if he was wounded? What if there were still mer we could save?

"How much chilyo paste do we have?" I asked without turning around.

"The jar I brought up is half empty," said Alexander, "but there's another jar in the kitchen."

I nodded and turned to face him. "Let's go see if we can find any survivors out there."

"Aye," said Mother. "That is something tangible we can do, no matter how helpless we feel."

We swam down the corridor to find Ti, Pippa, and Benjamin talking quietly in the front room. Or, rather, Ti talking *to* Pippa and Benjamin.

Pippa's eyes were still haunted, and Benjamin looked more grown-up and serious than I'd ever seen him.

I paused. Had Benjamin had to kill someone? Then the nausea rose up in my stomach. *I'd* killed someone. Two mer, in fact.

I, who had once decided to let Tor kill me rather than respond in violence, had taken the lives of two mer I didn't even know. All I knew about them was that they were part of an enemy army. Did they have families? Were they good mer caught up in a terrible system? What had I done?

The thoughts whirled in my head, and I couldn't stop them.

Ti glanced over at me, understanding in her eyes. "Stay, Jade. Listen to me."

Mother cleared her throat. "We're going to see if we can save any of the fallen Guard."

I closed my eyes. "I have to keep busy, Ti. I can't sit still with my thoughts. There may be time for that later, but right now . . . I just can't."

"I'll come with you," said Pippa. "To keep watch while you look. It's safer that way, and I'd like to be useful."

Benjamin started shaking violently all of a sudden. "I-I can't," he said. "I have to stay here. I'm sorry."

"You're going into shock," Ti said. "It's natural. I'll wait with you. You're going to be fine."

I had never taken Ti for a nurturer, but the gentleness in her countenance surprised me. Ti had seen death before. As a young harpy, before she began a life in Marbella, her people been slaughtered, and she had been one of the few survivors. She understood this better than any of us.

"Thank you," I said, my voice husky as I moved to the door. "We'll be back soon."

Alexander grabbed his head and winced.

"What is it?" I asked, alarmed.

He waved a hand. "It's nothing. I'm fine."

"Is your head bothering you? Your injury—"

"I said I'm fine."

But his face was pale.

"No, you're not," I said. "What if you get confused again? The blood is so thick out there you might not be able to find your way back."

"I'm not going to sit here and do nothing while you en-danger yourself in the canal. Did you see the sharks?"

"I saw one of them." I studied him. "Stay at the door with your weapon. Be prepared to let us inside at a moment's notice. That's what you can do to help."

He started to protest, but then he winced again and grabbed his head.

"I won't hear another word. Stay. Keep watch at the door."

He relented, taking hold of his knife. "I'll be here. Call out if you need help."

"I will." I leaned in and kissed him—a desperate kiss born of the need to feel something in the midst of all the destruction. With a final pulse of my gills in the relatively clean water of the house, I broke away from him, steeled myself, and opened the door.

The death in the canal felt like another twisting of a knife in my gut. There were so many bodies, Thessaloniken and Neptunian alike, strewn in front of our house. So much blood.

So much death. So much destruction. So much hate.

I would rather die than hate? Bah. I'd believed that once. But I was so tired. I just didn't know anymore.

Pippa, Mother, and I swam forward, close along the ground, searching the faces for any signs of life. I stopped to turn over the body of a mermaid, and I recognized her face from school. *Artemis.*

She'd been a few years older than I, so I didn't know her well, but it still came as a shock.

Body, after body, after body. Many looked familiar. For a few, I could summon their names. Some I didn't recognize at all. A few were floating in a macabre imitation of life rather than lying on the seafloor. I hadn't seen any sign of Maximus—or Tor, for that matter.

"I've found someone!" Pippa cried.

Mother and I rushed over to her. She knelt next to a pale merman with a deep spear wound in his stomach. He gasped when she grasped his hand.

Mother knelt over him and inspected the wound. She looked up at me sadly and shook her head. Then she bent over to look the merman in the eyes.

"What's your name, child?" she asked.

"Julius," he whispered.

Startled, I studied his face more closely and couldn't believe I hadn't recognized him. He'd been in my year in school. He must have just joined the Guard recently. And already dying for it.

"You're not alone, Julius. Go in peace," Mother said.

"Peace—" He gurgled.

"I'll stay with him until he passes." Mother glanced up at me. "Go on, and see if there's anyone we can save. Take the chilyo paste."

I bent down and plucked the chilyo paste out of her hand and then, with a final look at Julius, followed Pippa over the sea of the dead. A flash of movement caught my attention through the swirl of red, and I turned to the right and swam to a merman holding up his hand weakly. "Help," he said, trying to push himself up, and wincing. His chest and torso were free of wounds, but a wicked slash ran down his tail, almost all the way to his fin.

He would have a terrible recovery and might not swim well the rest of his life, but he would live if we staunched the wound and got him to safety.

I sank to the seafloor next to him, shuddering as I pushed a body out of the way. "I'm Jade," I said. "I'm going to put some chilyo paste over the wound to stop the bleeding, and then Pippa and I are going to take you inside my house where you can rest until it's safe to move you to the house of healing."

"Tychicus," he said through clenched teeth. "And thank you. There were just so many of the skubs."

"I know." I pulled the lid off the jar of chilyo paste. "Everyone fought bravely."

I scooped a handful of paste out of the jar and spread it across the wound in long, smooth strokes. He bit down hard on his lip but remained quiet. Once I'd coated the entire wound, I glanced down at his face. "You can't swim at all with that, can you?"

He shook his head. "Cleaved the muscle right in two, I think. But . . . " He gazed out over the destruction on the canal. "But I was lucky. Very lucky."

"How do you feel?" I asked.

"The wound hurts," he said. "Other than that, I'm pretty numb." He gazed at a dead mermaid next to him. "It's probably for the best for right now."

"Pippa," I called.

"Yes," she said from somewhere on the other side of the canal.

"Let's get him inside."

She jetted toward me and looked over the wound. "Let's each take an arm," she said. "I don't want to risk damaging his tail further."

"I appreciate that," he quipped.

We lifted him carefully, draped an arm over each of our shoulders, and began swimming back toward the house.

"Alexander," I called when we approached.

A scraping sound came from behind the door, and Alexander swung it open. "Found someone?"

Pippa and I carried Tychicus inside and handed him off to Alexander and Ti.

"Get him into a hammock so he can rest," I said. "We're going to see if we can find anyone else."

A sense of purpose drove each flick of my fin as I soared out the door and back into the bloody water. We'd done it. We'd helped someone. Maybe there was someone else we could still save.

I numbed myself to the horror as we swam back over the dead.

Silhouettes in the murky water reassured me that we weren't the only mer who'd had this idea. At least two other mer—maybe more, since I couldn't see far, were swimming through the carnage, looking for survivors to save.

Mother had left Julius's side and was swimming toward us, her face drawn and tired. "Let's keep at it," she said. "Before more Neptunians come and we lose the chance."

Face, after face, after face. Still no sign of Maximus. They were all blurring together now. I didn't know how many dead there were, nor did I know if I was swimming in circles, passing over the same bodies again and again.

A fin twitched, but the red-haired mermaid it belonged to showed no other signs of life. I bent over to check her pulse. Nothing.

Then, out of the corner of my eye, I saw another fin twitch, and I swam toward it before pulling up short. This mermaid was alive.

But she was Neptunian.

TWENTY-NINE

What do I do? I had not considered this possibility. The Neptunian turned her head to look at me, something almost like amusement curving her lips. She had bright crimson hair—at least it looked like it in this water—and a pretty face that seemed deeply cynical, like she'd seen too much pain to care anymore.

"Go ahead," she said in a voice that seemed almost lively. "Kill me. I'm dying anyway."

I searched her for the wound and found it on her tail, almost at her fin. I gasped when I look at it more closely. Her fin was nearly cleaved from her body, dangling from her tail by only one-third of the scales. A piece of armor that ran down her tail vertically had saved it from being severed altogether. But the wound wasn't bleeding profusely. It didn't appear to be fatal, though it was certainly disabling.

"You're not dying," I said.

She laughed. "I could swim again with enough treatment, but not well enough to go to war. Nor well enough to make it all the way back home, even if they'd take me. Which they wouldn't, after a dishonorable loss in battle." She stared up at the surface. "Just end it. My general would kill me if she found me here like this."

I followed her gaze. The overlander ships had formed a circle around our reef, and I imagined them preparing to throw nets into the water. Would it make a difference at this point?

"I'll help you," I said. "If you will swear an oath not to harm another soul here in Thessalonike."

She scoffed. "I don't want your pity."

"Do you want to die?"

She didn't answer at first, and I read the *no* in her eyes. "There's nothing left for me," she finally said. "I can't fight for the Neptunus Confederacy. I can't go home."

"You could stay here," I said.

This time she laughed aloud. "And your people would take me in? I'm no fool. Nor do I desire to be tortured. And I'm not so dishonorable as to defect."

"Very well." I swam over her to look for more survivors. Another dead. And another. And another.

And then I found the face I didn't want to see.

Maximus.

Maximus was dead, in my canal, a trident still lodged in his throat. My hands went numb. Not him too.

Gone.

I whimpered and pulled the trident from him as gently as I could and sank down to the seafloor. With my other hand, I reached out and closed his eyes. "Go in peace, Max."

New anger filled me, a hot, livid rage that threatened to tear me apart from within. Had the water grown even redder from Maximus's blood, or could anger color the very water around me? I grasped the trident between my fingers and flipped around to search out the Neptunian mermaid. She wanted death, did she? After all that had been taken from me, I could give her that.

But I stopped as soon as she came into view. Even in the depths of my anger, I couldn't kill in cold blood.

"Find a friend?" she asked with a smirk.

"Yes, as a matter of fact," I said, realizing I'd left the chi-lyo paste at her side. Perhaps I'd known all along that I was coming back for her. I swam toward her and set the trident just out of her reach, eyeing the perimeter around her for weapons and seeing none.

Would the chilyo paste help this wound? I was no physician, but it seemed as though it might. That it would be better than nothing, at least. Gently, I pressed the sliced edges of the fin together and set about putting a generous amount of chilyo paste around the tear.

"Are you . . . trying to heal me?" she asked, an edge in her voice.

"I'm going to save your life," I said. "You can choose to swear an oath to bring no more harm to anyone in the city or be tied up while you recover."

"What makes you think an oath will bind me?" she asked.

"You said you had too much honor to defect. Seems reasonable that you wouldn't back out of an oath."

"Well, you're right," she said. "And I am already sworn to the Neptunus Confederacy. I obey the orders given by the general and ask no questions."

"And what orders are you currently acting on?" I smeared another dab of paste on her fin.

A hammerhead brushed past my arm, and she and I both froze. It disappeared into the red haze. Perhaps it was already sated. I shuddered. "Pippa! Mother!" I called. "Shark."

Calls of acknowledgment came from somewhere closer to the house.

I looked back at the Neptunian. "You don't want to die."

She shrugged. "Of course I don't. But I seem to be rather out of options."

To my left came another scream. I squinted in that direction, trying to see, and I realized with a start that the choking blood had gotten so thick I was nearly blind. I extended my hand and couldn't quite make out my fingertips.

Click, click, click.

The sound I least wanted to hear. I'd heard that sound before. It was the call of a webbed-foot dragon.

And this one probably wasn't a baby.

"*Faex*," muttered the Neptunian.

I put my hand over her mouth lest she draw the dragon to us.

Then, all at once, a massive shape loomed out of the water, gliding toward me. A dragon.

I shrieked before I could stop myself and darted away into the blood-red water, begging the tides it would conceal me.

But the dragon remained close behind me, snapping at my tail. I cursed the choking water as I surged forward as fast as I could, trying to stay out of its snapping jaws. With a sharp turn, I tried to lose it. But it was almost upon me.

I made another quick turn and then swam upward and out toward the city wall. Maybe if I got away from the blood it would lose interest. But I had to make another turn to avoid its vicious teeth.

Then I heard a sound I almost couldn't believe.

A squeal. I knew that squeal.

A blur of gray shot past me, right at the dragon, and slammed into it at full force. The dragon let out a scream.

Kiki had come to save me. Somehow, she'd known. Had she . . . *followed* the dragon? Or somehow heard my shriek amid all the chaos in the city?

I sailed back toward my canal and down toward the seafloor as fast as I could, feeling amid the bodies for weapons. Any weapons. I found a spear and a trident and surged back upward.

That dragon wouldn't kill my dolphin if I had anything to do with it. Kiki screamed, but I didn't think she was in pain. She sounded angry.

Click, click, click.

I followed the noises until I saw them as shadows in front of me. I gripped the spear in my right hand and the trident in my left. I had two shots. And my aim had to be true, or I'd risk skewering Kiki.

"Hey!" I called at the dragon. Then more movement caught my attention from my left. A hammerhead.

Depths.

Kiki left the webbed-foot dragon behind and swam at the shark, bowling into its gills and knocking it off its trajectory toward me.

In front of me, the dragon charged. I steadied my gills and took aim, throwing the spear at the dragon's mouth. It lodged in its throat, but the beast kept coming.

Depths, depths, depths.

Suddenly, Mother was at my side, a trident in each hand. I hurled my trident, and it glanced off the dragon's nose.

"Swim!" I yelled.

But Mother's gaze was steely as she took aim with her first trident, sending it sailing directly into the dragon's eye. It let out a guttural scream and pulled up, swimming away from us and out toward the reef. It was over.

I trembled. Then I remembered. "Kiki!" I called, turning toward where I'd last seen her.

She whistled in response, and I swam in her direction.

"Jade, come back!" Mother called, but I ignored her.

I almost ran into Kiki. She was swimming at the hammerhead again, and she rammed into its gills just as I came upon her. The shark's movements had slowed, as though Kiki had injured it in the fight. Mother came up behind me, wielding the final trident. She extended it to me. "Would you like to do the honors?"

The shark wasn't moving now. I grasped the trident, rolled it between my fingers, and then skewered the hammerhead through the gills. The trident's tips emerged from the other side of the shark, the weapon firmly lodged in its flesh. Its fin twitched a little, and then it grew still, floating but almost imperceptibly sinking toward the seafloor.

Kiki nudged me, and I scratched her behind her dorsal fin. "Good girl," I cooed. "How did you know?"

She whistled.

I leaned over her and made a few clicks with my tongue, and she turned and soared back out toward the reef. But I wasn't under any illusion she'd gone far.

"Safe tides," I whispered.

Then I glanced at Mother and, wordlessly, we began the swim back down toward the seafloor.

"This way." Mother nudged me to the right.

"How can you tell?" I asked, squinting. My gills felt heavy in the toxic water.

"I just can," Mother said.

I shrugged and followed her lead, and sure enough, when we emerged out of the red haze, we found ourselves in our own canal, at our own door.

"Let's go in," said Mother.

I shook her off. "I'll be right back. Send Pippa if you find her." I turned and swam back into the canal.

Where had that Neptunian been? The blood had somehow grown even thicker, and I had to swim closer to the bodies now to distinguish their faces. Then I found her.

"You're still alive," she said, a hand-length from my face.

I tensed, startled, but reached down and grasped the tube of chilyo paste and inspected her wound again. "Yup. Took some work to remain that way. It'll probably take some work to make sure you remain that way, too."

She squinted at me. "Why do you care?"

"Because I have a penchant for trouble, and I'm bad at leaving things be. What's your name?"

"Does it matter?"

"Something to call you, then," I said. "Rather than *the Neptunian*, which is your current nickname in my head, and probably not the most original one I could have devised."

She hesitated. "You can call me Aenea, if you must."

199

"Thank you. Now, will you swear to do no more harm in this city unless your general gives you a direct command to the contrary?"

She tilted her head. "Aye. That I will swear. On the glory of Neptunus."

"Alright. Pippa!" I called.

Pippa emerged from the red murk a few moments later.

Another scream shattered the relative quiet. I wasn't sure what direction it came from, but I knew I didn't recognize the voice.

Pippa, Aenea, and I all looked back and forth wildly. Then another scream came. Again, I wasn't sure about the direction.

"Let's go," said Pippa. "Hurry." Then she looked at Aenea and paused. "Jade . . . what are you doing?"

"She's alive," I said. "And she needs our help."

Pippa pursed her lips. "Of all your starfish-brained ideas, Jade Cleopola, this may be the worst."

"We can't leave her to die."

"Yes, we can. That's what she would do to us. She chose her fate when she invaded Thessalonike with the rest of the Neptunians."

"I can hear you, you know," Aenea said.

"Look, I've talked to her. We have to do this. Now, before more sharks come. Do you trust me?"

Pippa scoffed. "Not even a little. But I'm also pretty sure we shouldn't stick around to see what those screams are about, and you're even more stubborn than your mother is. Come on. Grab her other arm. Let's go."

"Let's bring your fin up, gentle and easy like this," I said, curling Aenea's lower tail until she could put one hand on the tail and the other on her fin to hold the pieces together. She hissed, biting down hard on her lip, but didn't say anything.

"Can you keep hold of that while we carry you inside?"

"Aye," Aenea muttered.

Pippa and I eased her arms over our shoulders and began swimming to the right side of the canal as fast as we could. The homes were eerie silhouettes in the red water, but as soon as we reached the edge, I knew where we were.

"Five houses down," I said, motioning with my head. "That way."

Pippa cast a gentle current behind us to speed our way, and we passed one, two, three houses before mine came into sight.

"Almost there," I murmured.

"Why are you doing this? Really?" asked Aenea.

"I told you," I said. "It's because I don't know what's good for me."

"It's because she has a savior complex," muttered Pippa.

"Maybe that, too," I said. "I just don't like seeing anyone or anything hurt or alone."

My thoughts turned to Kiki. I hoped she'd made it back to the reef safely. One way or another, this would be over soon, and I'd be able to go find her. Unless they killed me.

Someone would survive. Me, or Pippa, or Benjamin, or Mother, or Alexander. And whoever it was would make sure Kiki was taken care of.

We reached my house and moved up the short path to the front door. This time, I knocked. Mother answered immediately, looking wan.

"You're back," she said. Then she stared at Aenea. "Jade Cleopola, what have you done?"

But she moved aside to let us enter.

Another scream. This time I thought it might be coming from our canal.

"Do you know what going on?" I asked. "The yelling?"

"More sharks, I think," said Mother. "But it could be"— she stared at Aenea—"more Neptunian attacks."

To her credit, Aenea shifted almost uncomfortably.

"Where can we put her?" I asked.

Mother looked down at Aenea's fin, and her eyes softened just a little. "Put her in your chamber. She'll be safe enough in your hammock."

And we'll be safe from her, seemed to come the unspoken thought. It would be difficult for a mermaid without the use of her fin to extricate herself from my hammock, make her way down the hall and to the first level of the house, and wage an attack.

Mother continued, "But make sure you take anything that could be used as a weapon out of the room. She's a Neptunian."

I nodded, and Pippa and I moved forward and swam upward through the vertical corridor. With a few more flicks of my fin, we reached my chamber and ducked through the privacy screen. "There." I eased Aenea onto my hammock. "Let's take a look at that fin again, shall we?"

The chilyo paste was still holding the injured scales together, and I was beginning to hope that it might heal without additional intervention. The cut had been clean, and I wasn't sure the physicians would treat her.

"Thank you," said Aenea. "You didn't have to do any of this. I-I don't know what to say."

I heard a chirrup, and A'a appeared in the doorway and skittered up my tail.

Aenea's jaw dropped. "You have a *dragon?*"

"This one's nicer than that other one was," I said. I carried A'a over to her and showed her his injured leg. "I found him trying to swim in open water. I could tell he wasn't going to make it if I didn't help."

"Told you she has a savior complex," Pippa muttered.

Aenea focused her gaze on me. "You're really not planning to turn me in for bounty money?"

I recoiled. "What? No."

"Jade has many faults," said Pippa, "but that's not her style. Might be mine, though."

I shot her a sharp look.

She held up her hands. "Sorry. Joking. Mostly."

Aenea glanced toward the window. "Well, I owe you thanks, then. And an apology for my suspicions."

"Just get some rest," I said. "I'll check on you in a while." With a dip of my head, I left through the privacy screen, Pippa at my side.

A sudden commotion rose up from outside and overhead—but not one that sounded like fear. Yells of . . . jubilation?"

"What's happening?" Pippa asked.

I bolted down the corridor and to the door. Throwing it open, I looked straight up at the surface. I couldn't see anything, but the water seemed just a little clearer, as though the blood was finally starting to dissipate. The cheers came again, definitely from higher up, toward the surface.

I turned to Pippa. "It must be the overlanders."

CHAPTER

THIRTY

What seemed like an interminable time later, the blood dispersed just enough for me to see the shadows at the surface. Definitely the overlanders. Massive nets were descending from the ships, swooping toward the city.

I also saw the sharks. Dozens of them, circling in and out of the cloud of blood.

My gills flared. Would the gambit work? Would the overlanders be able to pull Neptunians out of the water, or at least entangle them long enough for the Guard to drive them off?

A group of Neptunians soared upward from the city on their hippocampi and surged toward the overlander ships.

Oh, no.

I watched, feeling helpless as the Neptunians drew back their tridents and bashed at the hulls of one of the ships with stroke after stroke after stroke. They understood the battle tactic.

From this distance in the hazy water, I couldn't tell exactly when they managed to bore holes in the hull of the first ship. But once I saw it leave formation and set off in the direction of land, I knew they'd done it significant damage. They launched off from that ship and swam to the next-closest one.

Three of the Thessaloniken Guard swam after them to try to fight them off the ships, but they were pulled away by more Neptunians, who dragged them away and flung them at a group of hunting sharks. I couldn't watch as the Guard were torn apart.

Everywhere I looked, there was blood and death, and we weren't winning.

So this is how it ends.

Movement out of the corner of my eye caught my attention. A flash of teal. Carlina.

"Can I come in?" she asked, hovering at the spot where the pathway to our door intersected the canal.

"Sure." I moved aside to let her enter, and she swam toward me and into the house. With one final glance at the surface, I followed her. There was no more point in fighting. We wouldn't be able to win without the overlanders, and all the overlander ships were setting sail for shore.

Though the Guard might keep fighting for a time, it was over.

Maybe Aenea would put in a good word for us.

The magnitude of what had just happened pounded in my ears. We had lost. The Neptunians would rule over us now, no matter how cruel, or vindictive, or tyrannical they turned out to be. There was nothing we could do about it.

At least not yet. Maybe in time we could rise up. But maybe then they'd come back and wipe us all out.

Aunt Junia had died for nothing. It was that part that broke me somehow. That nothing would have changed if we'd stayed inside and not fought at all, except we'd still have Aunt Junia.

What a joke war was.

I eased into a hammock chair and turned to Carlina, "I'm glad to see you still alive."

"Me too."

"I suppose our escapade from a few days ago won't make a difference anymore," I said, tucking my hair behind my ears. "Elias will likely be killed or removed from power so the

Neptunians can install someone favorable to them. Maybe even one of their own."

"I expect so, yes."

"Are you here to hide somewhere safe until it settles?"

"If you'll have me. I . . . Faustus and I had a falling out."

"The more the better at this point. Though you may not want to go to the second level. It's practically a house of healing up there."

She raised an eyebrow in silent question, but I ushered her back to the kitchen. "We have food. We stocked up before the Neptunians arrived."

"Thank you," she said. "I—"

A great cry rose up from somewhere outside. I winced and bit my lip. It was agonizing to listen to the sounds of death, but what could we do? What was the point of fighting to the last mer when it was so clear we were outmatched? Why take more Neptunian lives, why give up our own lives, for nothing?

The noises grew louder. I tilted my head to listen. Something was different. But I couldn't quite put my fin on what it was.

I turned to find Alexander in the corridor, looking at me. He sensed it, too. Without a word, we darted to the door and tugged it open, searching the murky water for a sign of what was going on.

A mermaid sailed overhead, her hand stretched out behind her . . . no. Not a mermaid. *A naiad.*

Behind her came three others, their ethereal garments flashing crimson.

What the depths was going on?

"Pippa!" I yelled, my voice reaching a hysterical pitch.

"What?" Pippa called from behind me. "Get away from the door, Ja—" She came up behind us and ground to a halt.

A dozen more naiads soared overhead.

"James!" Pippa whispered. "Mira! They came!"

Something like hope filled me, chasing away the despair. "What do you mean, they came?"

Pippa laughed. "I-I don't know why. Or how. But they came back. They're here."

One of the naiads pushed his hands out and send a wall of water pressure smashing into a Neptunian who was charging a member of the Guard. The Neptunian and her hippocampus sank toward the seafloor three canals over, seemingly unconscious.

"Let's go," Pippa said.

"What . . . is happening?" I asked.

"The naiads are saving your city," she said. "Let's join them. Grab the tridents."

Going into battle the second time didn't feel quite so unnatural. Ti and Benjamin stayed back to keep an eye on Aenea, but Pippa, Mother, Alexander, and I zipped down the death-laden canal and around a corner, looking for a Neptunian to forcibly remove from the city.

It wasn't long until we found a group of three who were swimming down a neighboring canal and breaking down the doors of houses. "For Junia!" Mother cried, charging them.

And Maximus, I thought to myself as we clashed with the soldiers. Alone, we would have been outmatched by their superior training, but we had a secret weapon. As the Neptunians focused on us, Pippa feinted to the side and sent a long, slender water spear flying through all three Neptunians at once.

For Aunt Junia.

We swam down the rest of the canal and toward city center. It seemed like naiads were everywhere. The tides had turned. Hope rose in my chest. We could throw the Neptunians out of the city. We could win this battle and send them straggling home, never to return.

Pain sliced through my shoulder, and I turned to find a Neptunian drawing back his trident for another strike.

No, not a Neptunian. It was Octavian, wearing Neptunian armor.

I darted upward, out of the way of the trident's spikes. I glanced down at my shoulder. He'd mistimed his aim and only sliced into my skin with one of the spikes of the trident, but *depths* it hurt. I shifted my trident to my left hand and turned on him.

"Maximus is dead," I called.

He didn't flinch. "Is that my concern?"

"Why did you betray us?" I demanded.

Pain, maybe even uncertainty flickered in his eyes. "Because I was set up, and I had nowhere else to go." He raised his trident again, and I dodged out of the way when he hurled it at me. I tossed mine at him, but my aim wasn't strong with my left arm, and he plucked it out of the water.

I turned to slice through the water, away from him. When I turned around and looked back at him, he was sinking to the seafloor, a water-spear evaporating behind him.

Pippa had saved us again. She and I shared a brief nod, gratitude swelling in my chest.

"Toward the palace," said Mother. "That's where most of the fighting is."

I plucked a trident from a nearby body, and we surged forward, my right arm dangling at my side. "Surely, Elias isn't still there," I said as we swam.

A grim look overtook her face. "I wouldn't bet that Elias is still alive."

I swallowed. As much as I'd come to loathe him, I wouldn't wish death on him. How many had we lost? It had to be staggering.

We emerged on the palace grounds to find it teeming with battle. The Guard and naiads in full-throated combat against the Neptunians.

"Alright, Pippa," I said. "This is where your skills matter most. We'll watch your back."

Pippa started forming water-spears, sending one after another flying with deadly accuracy. We stood in a circle behind her, facing outward, daring anyone to come for her.

A dark-haired Neptunian that I vaguely recognized as the spy who had scoped out Thessalonike dropped in front of me from above. He drew his weapon, a long black sword— not a trident, like most of the Neptunians carried. I pitched my trident at him, but he dodged it easily, and it sank to the seafloor to his left. I moved back, weaponless. Mother and Alexander nodded at each other and surged at him in a joint attack, but he pushed back Alexander and deflected Mother, disarming her, and then turned his full attention back to Alexander.

"No!" I screamed, flying forward to throw myself between Alexander and the wicked-looking blade. I skimmed along the pointed edge, reaching out and grasping the blade to keep myself from being impaled. The sword tore into my hands and bit into the top of my hip bone. My vision went dark from the pain. I was barely aware of myself sinking to the seafloor, unable to see what was happening around me. I could still hear, but it sounded as though I were in deep water, far from the reef and everything that was happening on it. Down, down, I sank. How could I still be sinking?

Would I find Father down here?

More pain, in my side this time, but I wasn't concerned about it. My head felt fuzzy. Still sinking endlessly into nothingness, I fell asleep.

CHAPTER

THIRTY-ONE

I woke on a cramped hammock shoved between two other hammocks in a dark room. I didn't recognize the mermaids sleeping on them. Blinking, I struggled to remember where I was.

The last thing I remembered was . . . pain. Sinking into an endless void. Falling asleep. Had I died and woken up somewhere else?

No. Something about the atmosphere of this room, the contours of the walls, seemed unmistakably familiar. I had been here before. But my head was just so fuzzy.

And why did my palms hurt so depths much? I held them up to look at them and saw that they were both bandaged, a white cloth wrapped all the way around them.

My hands weren't the only things that hurt. My hip. My side. My shoulder. My head.

Flashes of memory flittered in my head. Fighting?

Oh. The Neptunians.

We'd fought the Neptunians. We were losing. And then the naiads came. Had we really won? I couldn't remember the end of the battle.

My chest felt heavy.

So heavy.

I tried to push myself up, but pain seared my whole body. For now, I wasn't getting up.

For now, I was tired.

For now, I would sleep.

⌒

When I woke again, my head felt a little clearer, though the pain in my body had only grown more intense. Perhaps whatever the physicians had given me to dull the pain was wearing off. I had no sense of how long I'd slept.

A jolt of panic ran through me. Where was my family? Alexander? Pippa? Were they okay?

A mermaid in a white wrap entered the room, swimming down the rows of hammocks inspecting the patients. Normally the rooms in the house of healing had one or two hammocks each. But there were at least a dozen mermaids in my room alone.

I held up my hand to signal to her as she passed by.

"Yes? Do you need something?" she asked. Her eyes were kind. Grandmotherly, almost.

"My family," I said. "Are they alright?"

"What's your name, my dear? I'll have someone go check on your loved ones."

"What happened?" I asked.

"What do you mean?"

"The battle."

"We drove out the invaders," she said, patience etched in every syllable.

"We?"

"The Guard."

I leaned back against the hammock, my mind whirring. Even after the naiads had saved our freedom, we still weren't giving them credit. *The Guard* had driven back the Neptunians, my fin.

My fin was something Aunt Junia would say. The memory

of Aunt Junia's death rushed over me anew, sending a fresh stab of pain through my heart. We'd won, but she was gone. And there was nothing we could do to bring her back.

But at least she hadn't died in service to a hopeless cause. Thessalonike had held the Neptunians back long enough for help to come, even though it wasn't the help we were expecting.

"My name is Jade Cleopola," I said.

"I'll send out an inquiry."

She continued on her round through the room, conversed quietly with another mermaid, and then left.

I was tired again, and the throbbing in my body had reached a crescendo.

I lay there, staring at the ceiling, unable to keep track of how much time had passed.

The physician re-entered the room and came to my side. "Your mother and fiancé are here in the house of healing, being treated. They're both going to be fine and will be released before you will be."

"My brother?" I croaked. "Benjamin?"

"He's uninjured and is waiting for your mother out front. There's a . . . strange creature with him."

I shot her a dirty look. "Marbellan Senator Ti, I believe you mean."

She held up her hands. "I meant no offense. I do believe the name was Ti, and she had an accent."

You could have said that in the first place.

"Is there a naiad anywhere?" I asked.

"Several . . . " she said slowly. "They're in another room together."

Depths. That's right. With all the naiads who had come to save Thessalonike, Pippa wouldn't stand out.

"I'm looking for a friend," I said. "Pippa Brook. Can you find out if she's alright?"

"I have other patients to attend to."

"Please. It's important. I swear she's the last person I'm asking after."

The physician's gills flared, but she nodded. "Fine. I'll see if any of the naiads here know anything about her."

"My brother might know!" I called, but she'd darted out the door, as if she were afraid I was going to change my mind and ask about someone else. There *were* other people I wondered about. Other friends and acquaintances. What had become of Carlina? Tor? Kora and Rhea? Crown Prince Elias, for that matter?

But I'd find out about all of them in time. For now, I just needed to know my family was safe. I counted the ridges in the coral ceiling, hoping to distract myself from the pain. It didn't help much.

At long last, the physician returned. "Your friend is fine. One of the naiads saw her after the battle ended. They're not sure where she is right now."

"Thank you," I said, but she was already out the doorway and down the corridor.

Only then did I let the relief flood me, and even though it exacerbated the pain, I let silent sobs shake my body.

THIRTY-TWO

Once four of the mermaids in my room were discharged later that day, the physicians allowed visitors to begin to come in. Mother, Alexander, and Benjamin were the first into the room.

"Jade!" Alexander said, rushing to my side and kissing me.

I returned his kiss with fervor, and Benjamin cleared his throat.

I laughed and broke away from the kiss. "You're alright," I said. "All of you are alright!"

Shadows darkened Mother's eyes. "Yes. We are."

Our grief for Aunt Junia rested heavily between us.

"What happened?" I asked. "I haven't been able to get much news in here."

"Together, the naiads and the Guard turned the tide against the Neptunians. More credit goes to the naiads, of course," said Alexander. "After you were injured, we brought you here. The Neptunians announced a retreat not a moment after we reached the house of healing."

A retreat.

"Will they be back, do you think?" I asked, playing with the netting on my hammock even though it hurt my hands. All of a sudden, I remembered why my hands hurt—I'd grabbed a naked blade to keep it from skewering me when I leapt in front of Alexander.

"I doubt it," said Mother. "Not after the losses they

sustained. But you never know. We'll be on the watch for them for some time."

"How many dead?"

"A lot. On both sides," she said. "We won't know the number for some time, I suspect, but I think everyone in the city knows someone among the dead."

I thought of Maximus's face among the bodies of the Guard, and another shot of pain jolted through me.

"Are you feeling alright?" asked Mother. "You were having a hard time with everything after the first battle."

I closed my eyes. "I feel detached from it, somehow. Like it wasn't me that shed blood, even though I remember doing it. I . . . don't feel any emotions about it." It startled me, somehow.

"Benjamin is much the same," she said. "I expect you'll have to cope with it later, but for now maybe it's best that you don't."

She was right, I suspected. "Did Elias survive?"

Mother glanced at the other mermaids, caution on her face. "The royal family is missing. Let us ask the tides they will be found unharmed." But from the expression on her face, I doubted there was much likelihood of that result.

After all, we'd won. Why would they still be missing if they were alive?

"All of them?"

"Crown Prince Elias, Princess Keira, and Prince Theo."

"Theo too?" My heart sank. "Who will inherit if they can't be found?"

"King Stephanos's niece, I suppose," said Mother. "Jessina."

I nodded. It made sense. Jessina was a little older than Elias, perhaps thirty or thirty-five. I didn't know her well, but I'd always liked her.

If we had to have a monarchy, she seemed like a good enough choice to rule. Carlina wouldn't be happy, and some part of me had hoped that a democracy would emerge out of the rubble of the battle. But Jessina on the throne would be good enough.

Sadness rippled through me when I thought about Theo, though. I gazed up at the ceiling. So much death. So much loss.

"Well, then," I said. "When can I get out of here?"

Mother laughed. "You don't change, do you?"

"Well, I hope I've changed. For the better, through all of this. Oh! Pippa. Where is she? I got the news that she's safe, but no one knew where she was."

Mother tilted her head. "I'm not sure either. I saw her after the Neptunian retreat, but not in the last couple hours."

Benjamin floated forward. "She said something this morning about going out to the reef to check on Kiki for you."

I don't deserve Pippa as a friend. I couldn't believe her thoughtfulness. She knew how much Kiki meant to me, and for her to make sure that Kiki was taken care of, even with everything going on . . . I would be so sad to see her go.

The ghost of a hope that she might stay now nudged at me. Were the naiads back for good? If they stayed in Thessalonike, we would treat them with honor this time.

But even I knew the thought was optimistic. Bigotry was hard to wash away. Even if we paid lip service to the great aid the naiads had given us, it couldn't erase the years of practice we had in treating them unfairly. Even if the injustice manifested itself with more subtlety than before . . . I couldn't ask Pippa to continue to put herself through that. Not after she'd set her heart on going back to the rivers.

No, Pippa would leave us soon. And I'd wish her well with all my heart.

⌒

A week later, though the pain was still constant, I found myself hovering outside the house of Maximus's mother, an elegant wrap in my hands. I thought the color would suit her. I knocked.

Tor answered the door. "Yes?"

"Oh . . . I didn't know you were here." I held up the wrap. "I've come to bring Mariana a mourning gift."

"Ah," he said, his expression downcast. "I'd wondered if you knew. I thought about coming to bring you the news, but . . ."

He didn't need to finish the sentence. Our history was complicated to say the least.

"I saw him . . . after," I said, my insides twisting.

"Mariana will be grateful for your thoughtfulness." He reached out to take the wrap, and I handed it to him. "She's asleep right now. Hasn't slept all week, so I don't want to disturb her."

"Of course not," I said. "You're taking care of her, then?"

He nodded. "Neither of us have anyone else. She's lost her sons. I've lost my parents. It won't be for long, but I want to make sure she gets through the worst of it."

Compassion filled me. "Your father died?

"No."

A clownfish zipped around my head, a rare sign of life in the city these days.

"Are . . . you okay?" I asked.

He bit down hard on his lower lip. "Why do you care?'

"Because I'm not sure you have very many people left who do."

"I don't," he said shortly. "And I don't know why Maximus died and I lived."

"What do you mean?" I tilted my head.

"Maximus was a good merman."

I remained quiet but nodded, encouraging him to continue.

"Why does Maximus die, and I survive? Why does the murderer survive the battle and the devoted soldier perish?" His voice reached a high, desperate pitch. "And the crown prince announced pardons for anyone who participated in the battle and killed a Neptunian, so I don't even finish out my sentence. I'm free. To move around the city, to work, to rejoin the Guard if I want to. After what I've done—"

"Tor—"

"I should have been the one to die. It was what I expected. A way to atone for my sins. To redeem myself." He clutched the doorframe, his fingers trembling. "I. Should. Have. Died. Not Max."

The answer came to me in a moment. "So now you have the hard work of living ahead of you. Of living differently. Better. Of taking the change that's begun in your heart and working it out day in and day out. Making it permanent. Maybe that's a better story than dying in battle to absolve your sins."

"What do I have left?" he spat.

"You have life. And the chance to write your future. It's a gift. Take it."

He shook his head from side to side, like he was trying to clear his churning thoughts.

"Become the merman you want to be. Like Maximus."

"Go in peace." He closed the door in my face.

I floated backward away from the house. I didn't know what would become of Tor, if he'd be able to channel the guilt that wracked him into change. I hoped he would. But that wasn't my responsibility.

It was up to Tor.

Two days later, I took Alexander out on the reef to re-introduce him to Kiki. We didn't bring A'a with us. I wanted Kiki to get used to things being normal again, to me coming out to visit her several times a week, before I persuaded her to accept a webbed-foot dragon. Even a baby one.

"I think things are finally settling down," I said to Alexander as we swam alongside Kiki, skimming over the seagrass and then upward toward the surface. "Not going back to normal, exactly. But . . . getting easier again. You know? Like we're on a reef again instead of treading in deep water."

He scratched Kiki up near her dorsal fin. "After they found the bodies of Elias and Theo and declared Jessina the crown princess, it seemed to settle everyone. Nothing like an existential threat from the outside to bring the mer together. Even the anti-monarchists aren't protesting her coronation."

I chuckled. "For now. Give it six months, and they'll be rioting again. I'm sure of it."

"You're probably right." He sounded distant, and the strokes of his fin grew sharper. "And Barnabas dead, too. The old order really is coming to an end."

While I didn't wish the worst on anyone, I couldn't muster any sympathy for Barnabas. Not after the way he'd tried to twist a knife in all our backs. And especially not after what he'd done to Orua. In the aftermath of the invasion, her attacker had claimed his pardon and confessed: he'd been hired by Barnabas to attack Alexander in the canal and Orua when she was guarding me. All to destabilize us further so that Mother wouldn't be able to reinsert herself with the crown prince.

Beyond despicable

Alexander still seemed pensive.

"What's wrong?" I asked as we skimmed the surface.

"What'll happen now? Thessalonike's still the same as it always was. The nobles divided from the working class."

I grasped his hand, and we both let go of Kiki and began sinking toward the reef together. "You and I will face that together. If it scandalizes the nobles, it scandalizes them. If it means we have to move to a different part of town and carve out a life as laborers, we'll make it work. It will be hard. But it will still be a good life. I just want to be with you."

"Are you sure?"

I spotted something in the coral below us and released his hand so I could swim downward to inspect it. A small pile of red coral pieces, carved in small circles, lay on top of the rock. Left there by someone. A Neptunian? A naiad? I sifted through them and picked up two that seemed like the right size.

Yes. I smiled. It just felt right.

"Alexander." I gripped the rings and swam upward until I could look him in the eyes. I tried to bite back a giddy smile. "We've known each other since we were young children. You were my best friend for so many years, and when you left school—left me—you took a part of me with you. When I found you in the naiad quarter that day, it was like my heart began to piece itself back together. I fought that feeling, and gave into panic, and lost you again. But that was the biggest mistake of my life. You and I belong together, and I want to face the future, whatever awaits us, at your side. Marry me?" I held out the larger of the two rings.

He reached out and took it, wonder on his face, and slipped it on his finger. Then he reached for the other ring and set it in his palm.

"Jade, I . . . I don't have a fancy speech, but I love you and don't ever want to let you go. Let's spend the rest of our lives together, no matter what the future brings. Marry me?"

I held out my hand, and he slipped the coral circle over my knuckle. It fit perfectly.

Kiki squealed above us, and I flew into Alexander's

220

embrace. His arms encircled me, and his lips found mine, kissing me until I felt dizzy.

Against all the odds, we'd found our happily-ever-after.

CHAPTER

THIRTY-THREE

We played on the reef with Kiki, giddy, until nearly midday. When we returned home, giggling and trying to suppress our overflow of joy, Mother glanced at the rings, and I thought I saw the expression on her face shift ever-so-slightly, like she was holding back a small smile. She said only, "Your father would be pleased."

It was the best thing she could have said.

I squeezed Alexander's hand.

Then Mother's face grew serious. "The Crown Princess would like to see you and me, Jade."

I drew back. "Whatever for?"

Mother shook her head. "I'm not sure. The message came while you were on the reef. I'm glad you came back when you did—I was beginning to wonder whether I was going to need to send Benjamin after you."

Tension pulled at my shoulders. Surely, we weren't to be punished. We'd fought for Thessalonike like most of the other mer in the city. Jessina was honoring Elias's amnesty.

So what could she want with us? Mother wasn't in her inner circle. It seemed unlikely that she was to be reinstated to her prestigious position as advisor. Besides, if a royal advisorship were the purpose of the meeting, why summon me?

In fact, Mother had spent the last few days inquiring about available positions among her friends. The death toll had been high—fifteen hundred mer dead, only half of that

222

number members of the Guard. In the wake of such devastation, jobs were inevitably plentiful, and Mother had her pick.

Mother said she'd find a position for me as well. If we were lucky, she'd even find something for Alexander.

Assuming Jessina wasn't about to pronounce our doom.

"When are we to go?" I asked.

"Before low tide today," she said, her voice even.

I glanced at the tide glass. We didn't have to leave immediately but neither could we linger for long.

"Can we get it over with?" I asked, picking at a fingernail. "I'm going to be worrying about it until we learn what she wants."

Mother chuckled darkly. "You read my mind. I'll go get my cloak. Want one?"

"Sure," I said, my gaze wandering toward the window.

Mother swam back toward the kitchen.

"Hey." Alexander reached out and massaged my neck. "We've already survived such dark and broken tides. The crown princess can't say anything to you that compares to what we've just endured."

He said it with such certainty, but it didn't bring me much comfort. He couldn't know that. Not really.

But we always had Marbella to flee to.

Pippa had glowed when she'd brought me the news about what had happened—about how and why the naiads had come. As soon as three-quarters of the Neptunian army left for Thessalonike, the naiads had risen up against the remaining invaders—and wiped them out.

The Marbellan senate was again in control, albeit much reduced after a short period of harsh Neptunian rule. But somehow, against all odds, Chancellor Ava Kamora had survived her imprisonment, and when the naiads liberated the city, she was rescued and restored to her former position. Special elections were being called in Marbella soon, said the naiads, to restore the senate to its full size. I suspected that many naiads would be among the newly elected senators.

I was relieved to hear my friend Claira had survived as well.

And then the naiads had followed the Neptunians to Thessalonike, to fall on them in the heat of battle and decimate their numbers so that Marbella would continue to be a place of safety.

Pippa had laughed. "They had no love for Thessalonike, but they saw the danger the Neptunians posed to everyone in the ocean if they were not given a harsh rebuke and sent on their way. After so much time living in Thessalonike, my people were done with tyrants."

Quillpricks ran down my spine. Regardless of their motives, I was so, so glad they came when they did.

Benjamin swam down the corridor from the second level, A'a perched on his shoulder. He darted over to give me a hug, and I relaxed as I pulled him into my arms. He was safe. He would be safe.

"Notice anything different?" I asked, a grin on my face.

He stared at me. "Um . . . no?"

I held up my left hand, showing off the ring.

His jaw dropped, and he glanced at Alexander for confirmation. Alexander clicked his tongue and pointed to the ring on his own hand.

"Yeah!" Benjamin pumped his fist. "Alexander is going to be my brother for real?"

"For real," Alexander said with utmost solemnity, though I had the sense that he was holding in his laughter.

"And you guys are sure this time?" Benjamin asked, his face serious.

In answer, I leaned over and gave Alexander a kiss on the cheek.

Benjamin screwed up his face in disgust. "Stop that."

"I thought you were happy we're engaged," I said.

"I am." He mimed gagging. "I just don't want to have to see you guys *kissing*."

Mother reappeared from down the hallway, a cloak in each hand. "Ready, Jade?"

"As ready as I'm going to be, I suspect." I reached out and took the cloak from her, and then wrapped it around my shoulders. I wouldn't hide my face today. Nor ever again, I hoped.

Mother glanced at Alexander. "Make sure Benjamin finishes his schoolwork?"

Benjamin groaned. "School just started up again yesterday."

"And I don't want you falling behind," Mother said in a fierce voice, but her gaze was nothing but affectionate. "My name doesn't mean the same thing in this city as it did when King Stephanos was on the throne. You children will have to make your own way now, and that means you will do well in school, Benjamin Nicopolos."

"We'll see how this meeting goes," I muttered.

"Yes," Mother said grimly. "We will see indeed."

After a final kiss on Benjamin's forehead, Mother ushered me out the door and onto the canal. No sooner had we turned than I caught a glimpse of Pippa coming toward us.

"Pippa!" I cried, waving at her and swimming steadily in her direction.

"Hi, Jade."

When I reached her, she took both my hands in her own. "I've come to say goodbye."

My heart ached, as if it were sinking over the drop-off and into the fathomless deep. "Have you decided to go back to Marbella with the others? Or are you still planning to look for a river system?"

"I'm going back to the rivers," she said. "I'm bringing along a couple friends."

I let go of her hands and pulled her into an embrace. "I'd ask you to stay, but that wouldn't be fair to you."

"I won't mourn anything I leave behind in the city except for Anna, you, and your family," she said. "I'm . . . excited for this adventure."

"Tides keep you safe. Go in peace."

"Peace be upon you."

"Have you told the other naiads yet?" I asked.

She shook her head. "I'm on my way there next. They're departing for Marbella tomorrow. Senator Ti will be going with them."

"Tell them thank you. For saving us," I said.

She gave me a wry smile. "I will."

"I know, I know." I waved my hand. "They didn't owe us anything. It was primarily about ridding this corner of the ocean of the Neptunians so that they could live in peace in Marbella. But I'm grateful for it nonetheless."

"I'll miss you, friend."

"Oh, me too. Me too." I hovered in silence for a moment, and then added. "Send word, if you ever have a chance, that you've found a new home and are safe."

"I will."

Mother touched my shoulder. "We have to go, Jade. Pippa, I'm so grateful for you. You've saved our lives many times over. You've been our most faithful friend in the midst of all the horror. Thank you."

"Thank you," said Pippa. "I'll miss you, too, Lady Cleo."

After Pippa and I shared a final hug, Mother and I continued on our way. At the corner, I turned around to look back at Pippa, but she'd already jetted away.

Mother and I swam toward the palace, and I took in the destruction that was still evident in every canal. The blood had fully dissipated, but the signs of the violence— broken doors, shattered coral, ruined structures—would take months to fully repair.

Three of the pink-and-teal spires had been broken off the top of the palace, giving it the look of a ruin. There wouldn't be any way to repair that. They'd have to shave the rest of the spires off. The scar the Neptunians had left on the silhouette of the city would be permanent.

We swam into the rubble-strewn courtyard and along the side of the palace until we reached the entrance of the court. Two members of the Guard were stationed outside. One of them, a purple-haired mermaid with a slim build, held up a hand. "The crown princess is in a meeting with her advisors. You'll have to wait."

"Thank you, Allia," said Mother, though her cheeks flushed red. I didn't think she'd ever been denied entrance to the court before, and the reminder of her loss of station had to sting.

We waited in the nearby coral garden, which had somehow remained untouched in all the fighting. It was devoid of animal life—the little seahorses that normally flitted from feeder to feeder had fled in the chaos and blood and not yet returned—but the coral and plants were beautiful as always. It was a welcome sign of life, of normalcy, in the midst of so much change.

"What are you thinking?" I asked Mother as she studied a blue anemone.

She didn't turn her head. "That I'm so glad my children are safe. That I hope I can keep you that way."

"What are you afraid the crown princess might say?"

"I don't know. And that's what troubles me. I can't fathom what's brought us to her notice."

"Well, you were well-known as King Stephanos's advisor. We know her, though not well. It's not as though she's unaware we exist."

"But why does she want to have a conversation with us? To offer a warning, perhaps?" Mother scuffed her fin along the sandy seafloor.

"In the worst case, she wants to make an example of us," I said. "But I don't think that seems like something she'd do."

"It's hard to know how power will change someone."

"Did Benjamin say anything about how school went yesterday?" I asked, grasping at anything to change the subject to safer waters.

She nodded. "A little. I don't think the other kids tormented him, like they did in the days leading up to the trial. Everyone is still in shock. Still in the *we're-in-this-together* stage."

"I hope that will last for some time," I said.

"I do, too," she murmured.

"I wonder what happened to Aenea?"

We'd hidden the Neptunian soldier for five days after the battle ended, but the day they brought me home from the house of healing, we'd found my window open and Aenea gone. With such a wound, she couldn't swim far, though she'd sliced a swath out of my hammock—I suspected to bind her fin with the netting.

We'd probably never know what had become of her.

I wanted things to end more cleanly, like the stories of old. When victory was declared, and everything was right again, good triumphant and evil punished, no loose threads hanging off the net. But it probably hadn't been like that when those stories were lived out, in flesh and scales and blood. We just told them that way because it made us feel like life made more sense.

"Lady Cleo, Lady Jade," called Allia, "Crown Princess Jessina will see you now."

THIRTY-FOUR

Jessina was short to begin with, and she looked even shorter sitting in the unassuming chair beneath the throne. But despite her stature, every inch of her looked regal and imposing. This was not a mermaid who took her duty lightly.

As Mother and I approached her hammock chair, Jessina turned her attention to us. Her piercing brown eyes appraised me, as if she could see straight through me.

"Lady Cleo, Lady Jade. Thank you for coming."

My heart beat fast as I dipped my head in acknowledgment.

"I'll get to the point," she said. "Because I'm sure you're wondering why you're here. Lady Cleo, you served my uncle faithfully for many years. I thank you for that. As I have gathered my advisors around me, I have determined your services will not be needed in that role in my court."

Mother nodded, her face blank. "Yes, Your Highness."

"Nevertheless," said Jessina, "this throne has overlooked injustices that I believe ought to be rectified. I believe you and I are of the same mind on that."

"Yes, Your Highness," Mother murmured.

"One particular concern that has weighed on me for weeks now—since not long after that peculiar trial for Tor Felicipolos—is the fate of the naiads whom Lord Felix sold into slavery. Five were sold before his scheme was uncovered, so far as the evidence suggests. One was discovered by the diplomatic delegation to Marbella. One we were able to recover and reunite with her people when Elias made a deal with Felix's overlander contacts to assist us in fighting the Neptunian imperialists. Her freedom was paid for by the seizure of some of Felix's assets."

This was news to me. Very good news.

"But three are still missing. This is not a crime our ancestors would take lightly, and I believe that not rectifying it would bring shame on our city and our memory in the generations to come. *Particularly*, after the naiads proved to be our salvation. Now that the tides have seen fit to entrust me with responsibility for the city, I will not let these naiads' fate be a stain on my reign."

"I'm so pleased to hear it, Your Highness," said Mother.

"I have brought you and Lady Jade here to inform you of your commission," said Jessina, "if you are willing to take it."

Realization dawned on me, and a smile spread across my face.

"I would like the two of you to spearhead the effort to recover the three remaining naiads. You can work with the inspectors and the diplomats as needed, and I will see that any merchants with relevant connections cooperate as needed. You will report directly to me, and this mission shall continue until every last naiad who was sold is accounted for and given the opportunity to return here or to be escorted safely to Marbella. Will you accept this mission?"

"Yes!" I exclaimed. Then I glanced sheepishly at Mother.

"Yes," said Mother more serenely, with an amused expression on her face. "Jade and I would be delighted to take on this task. It will be an excellent start to Jade's career, and quite meaningful work for both of us."

"I am glad to hear it," said Jessina. "You will begin in exactly one month to give the inspectors time to make a final report of the dead. At that time, I will summon the chief inspector and Lavinia, along with the two of you, to a meeting here to discuss the best way to proceed. Go in peace."

"Peace be upon you," we said in unison. We each bowed and then turned to swim toward the door to go back home.

I couldn't believe what the tides had brought us. A start to my career. An opportunity to finally set this wrong to right. And I was to do it alongside Mother.

As soon as we swam into the water outside, I grabbed Mother by the shoulders and spun us both in a circle. "Can you believe it?" I asked, my voice an octave higher than normal. Then I let her go and darted toward the canal.

"Where are you going?" called Mother.

"Pippa needs to know the good news before she leaves for the rivers!"

⌒

The day after the naiads left, I woke Benjamin as the first light of dawn trickled into the city.

He threw an arm over his eyes in true dramatic fashion. "Go away. It's too early. Are you trying to kill me?"

"Come on," I said. "Let's go onto the reef today. Cut class."

He moved his arm and peeked up at me. "Really?"

"Really. I'll take all the blame when Mother gets mad. Come on. Hurry up. We're sneaking out before she can stop us."

A'a climbed out from underneath the blanket covering Benjamin and stretched his front legs all the way out, his backside swaying.

"Well, hi there." I reached out and scratched his chin, and he rubbed his cheeks against my finger. "He's really taken to you," I said to Benjamin.

Benjamin blinked a few times and nodded.

Then A'a climbed up the netting to the top of the hammock, curled up, and went back to sleep.

"Come *on*." I tugged at Benjamin's arm. "I have a pouch full of crabcakes and sweet puffs. We'll eat breakfast on the reef."

"*Fiiiine*," he said. "Let me get changed."

I flew downstairs and left Mother a tablet on the table.

I took Benjamin to the reef for the day. Sorry. I'll make sure he gets caught up on schoolwork. Love, Jade

Benjamin floated downstairs, still bleary-eyed, and I grabbed his hand and pulled him out the door. The sunrise cast an orange tint on the water as we blew past the Guard at the city gates. There were more than usual stationed along the wall. Probably would be for years to come.

Benjamin and I skimmed over the coral reef, passing over a school of silver fish and a forest of branching coral before reaching the spot where I often called Kiki.

"Kiki!" I called.

Somewhere in the distance, she squealed in response.

Benjamin squinted in every direction, looking for her. He jumped, startled when she appeared suddenly over his left shoulder. I laughed.

"Grab her fin! Let's go!" I called.

We each grabbed one side of Kiki's dorsal fin and sailed up toward the surface, launching into the air just as the sun broke over the horizon. I glanced down at my red-coral engagement ring as we plunged back beneath the waves. I let go of Kiki, and they continued forward while I sank down toward the seafloor and looked back at Thessalonike.

The broken spires of the palace looked decrepit, and even from here, I could see the rubble of the shattered pieces of the wall. So much violence, so much hate had decimated us. And no doubt, in time, we'd have to fight against the old divisions when they sought to destroy us all over again. The future was uncertain. It always would be. But, for now, we would rebuild our city, and our lives.

I looked down at my ring again, and then gazed at Benjamin and Kiki, soaring up toward the surface again.

"Come on, Jade!" Benjamin called.

Joy bloomed in my core, spreading down my arms and all the way to each of my fingertips. Yes, time to rebuild.

We'd already started.

A NOTE FROM THE AUTHOR

Did you like the book? I'll be forever grateful if you take the time to leave a review on Amazon, Goodreads, Barnes and Noble, Kobo, or iBooks. Reviews are the number-one way you can help other people discover the authors you love, and each and every review supports us on our journey to bring you more stories. A review doesn't have to be long or detailed—just honest! I'm so thankful for each and every one of you.

Go deep!

ACKNOWLEDGMENTS

With every new book, I'm reminded again that publishing is truly a team sport. I'm so grateful for the people on my team.

My editors, Keith Osmun, Stephanie Monk Guido, and Ben Guido. This book is so much better because you were part of it.

My cover artist, Kirk DouPonce, who never ceases to amaze me.

My formatters, Chris Bell and Kella Campbell, and their phenomenal attention to the sorts of details that would overwhelm me.

My wonder women, Lindsay, Avily, and Sarah, for keeping me sane, renewing me creatively, and always encouraging.

So many friends who make my life better, especially Stephanie, Jessica, and Chris.

My husband, whom I adore.

And most of all, my readers—you are all my favorites, and I'm so glad you've come with me on this journey. Go deep!

Made in the USA
Columbia, SC
09 July 2019